The
Lost
Manuscript

Breanna Bright

Outskirts Press, Inc.
Denver, Colorado

The Lost Manuscript
All Rights Reserved

Outskirts Press
http://www.outskirtspress.com

ISBN-10: 1-59800-545-6
ISBN-13: 978-1-59800-545-5

Outskirts Press and the "OP" logo are trademarks belonging to Outskirts Press, Inc.

Printed in the United States of America

DEDICATION

This is for my parents, Paula and Steven.
They did everything but write the book.
I love you with all my heart.

PART ONE

PROLOGUE

(1920)

The only light came from a candle. It was tall, red and sticking out of a green champagne bottle, the red wax ran slowly down the candle to the bottle, and fell onto the small wooden desk. The only piece of furniture in the room. The flame cast a small glow about the room, and formed eerie shadows on the bare walls. A small mouse quickly ran across the bare wooden floor to the other side where it might fine shelter in the hole in the woodwork. The scraping of it's feet on wood was the only sound in the room. But if you listen closer you would hear the gentle breath of a man sitting at the desk. The man was not very tall, but not that short either. He had thick dark hair that played about his face, with very dark green eyes, so dark that at a distance they looked brown, even black. His skin had a dark complexion, in fact everything about him seemed rather dark.

He bent over the desk quietly, and nervously. In his large hand he gripped a black pen. The tip of it floated a few centimeters above a small wrinkled piece of paper. The man closed his eyes and wiped the sweat from his brow, his right hand holding the pen never wavered.

The pen slowly dipped downward and touched the white

paper. But it did not start to move. It remained on the paper and a small ink spot started to form. But the man only stared at the paper deep in thought. While the candle light played across his face.

The man breathed deeply, this seemed to be the signal to begin. His pen ran across the paper forming small curving words. They ran on down the paper filling it up well. At the bottom of the page he signed his name. He stared at the paper for a long time, not reading it though, just looking at it, as though making sure it still existed, as if it would disappear at any moment.

Light suddenly filled the room as a car quietly rode up and the headlights shined through the window, then disappeared. The man sat as still as a cat stalking it's prey. The room was as silent as death. Then a small thump, of a car door slam broke the quiet night. There was a squeak of wood as the man stood up and blew out the candle. He walked across the room in two steps not making a sound. With a quick jerk a small board on the floor was lifted and the man disappeared underneath it. Just a moment later the door to the small room opened and a very tall man stepped in.

He was rather thin for a man of his age. His hair was a light brown and cut into a short buzz. Two small hazel eyes studied the dark room carefully. He stepped into the room lightly, the boards creaked under a pair of large black boots. The second man walked up to the desk and reached into his pocket, pulling out a small match book. There was a snap when the match hit the paper and a small flame appeared. The man placed it to the candle and looked around once again. He looked at the desk and picked up the small piece of paper. He scanned it briefly then placed it back on the desk.

A third man now entered the room. He was black, with no hair and rather large brown eyes.

"Burn it," The tall man whispered. He then turned and left the room, his large black boots creaking on the old wood. The third man walked up and picked up the piece of paper. He placed it up to the candle's flame. The fire started to eat at the paper greedily, the white became brown, then black, and then ash fell off onto the desk.

The man heard a faint noise. He turned, and did not comprehend the first man. The man with dark green eyes raised his fist and brought it down hard and purposely on the third man's mouth and nose. The third man clutched his face and groaned in pain, he felt blood on his hands.

The first man grabbed his shoulders and brought his knee up into the man's stomach. The man coughed and fell to the floor. The first man lifted his foot and shoved it upward into the third man's face. He jerked backward, fell onto his back and was still. The first man turned and quickly put the flame out with his hand, he had saved the paper.

He reached under the desk and pulled out a small, thin, leather briefcase. He took the burnt paper gently and put it inside on the outer pocket. The man threw the briefcase out the window. It fell through the dark air and landed in the lap of a sleeping homeless man.

The Hobo wore a dirty travel coat, and a large hat that covered his face. When the briefcase landed in his lap he grabbed the handle and stood up, and started walking down the sidewalk. The light from the candle disappeared and shadow took over the small window of the building. The Hobo walked on down the dark and deserted sidewalk until he came to a post office.

Once inside the Hobo removed his dirty travel coat revealing a long clean trench coat, he took off his hat letting his long dark hair fall out past his shoulders. He pulled the hair into a ponytail and put his clothes in the trash can. He walked across the empty room, jumped over the counter and came out the back, still carrying the briefcase.

He walked on down the street until he came to the end of town. Here he untied a horse from a tree and rode off down the country road, never stopping his horse, and never dosing in the saddle.

By the first morning light he had reached his destination. The sunlight revealed a beautiful country side, with rolling green hills, clear fishing lakes, yellow dirt roads, and a never-ending blue sky.

The man stopped his horse in front of a large white house. He walked to the front door and pushed the door bell once, just once.

A minute later the door opened. An elegant, graceful woman smiled kindly at him, her blond hair was worn short to her shoulders, and her lovely blue eyes gleamed in the morning light. He said nothing, simply held out the briefcase. The woman took it, and her smile disappeared. The man nodded his head and left. He mounted his horse and rode off down the road. The woman watched him, then looked down at the briefcase.

"Ink," She whispered.

"Pardon Miss?" The maid appeared at her side, awoken by the doorbell. The blond woman handed the briefcase to the maid.

"Take it up to the attic please," She said simply.

"Will you not open it?" the girl asked cautiously.

"I have no wish to see what it contains," she said, "do as I say." She took the case, and walked silently upstairs. She was a young girl of fifteen, she was rather thin, her long blond hair was her best feature when it came to looks, it was a lovely golden and waved down past her shoulders, and her silvery blue eyes where filled with curiosity and wonder.

Her bare feet were silent on the carpeted floor, as she made her way to the second floor of the house. Here she reached upward, standing on tiptoe and grasped a thick rope. When she pulled it, a piece of the ceiling came downward, connected to the ceiling on the inside was a stiff and short ladder. The girl pulled it until the ladder touched the floor, and then climbed upward to the darkened attic.

At the top she instinctively reached her hand to the right of what was now a hole in the attic floor, to grasp a short white candle lying on the floor. She reached into the pocket of her dress and pulled out a match book. She struck the match and lit the candle, filling the small room in a comfortable glow.

The candle light revealed all the wonders of the attic, large wooden chest filled with unknown items, piles upon piles of books, old furniture as well, moth eaten couches, and small wooden rocking chairs. The attic held many things, many secrets, and many stories.

The girl walked carefully across the wooden floor, clutching the mysterious briefcase and the glowing candle. She walked down to the far end of the attic to a small dusty corner that had not yet been occupied by any of the attic's holdings.

The girl bent down to her knees and placed her candle on the floor beside her. Her mind ached with curiosity as to what the briefcase contained. She had always been a curious girl, with a wild imagination, and she deserved better than the life of a maid, but some things cannot be helped.

She glanced over her shoulder at the open hole of the attic floor, all was silent down there. Her fingers played over the strap of the briefcase, then clutched it but did not move. Her face harden, and with a deep breath she released the strap and peered into the case. But this part was empty. There were two other pockets on either side of the briefcase.

She began to open the pocket, but a call from the hallway caused her to gasp in fear. "Bay!"

Bay's heart skipped a beat and she sucked in her breath, she glared at the empty attic opening, then peered longingly at the leather case. With a heavy sigh she picked up her candle and made her way back to the opening. She placed the candle back in it's original place by the opening. With a quick breath the flame went out putting the attic in darkness once again. Bay hesitated at the top of the stairs looking back at the far corner where the mysterious case now lay. Bay looked downward with depression, and sighed once again. She walked down the ladder and pushed the ceiling back to it's place, plunging the attic into darkness, and leaving the briefcase alone, and unknown.

Chapter One

It was the month of May, the weather was warm, and the air was clear. The sun was just starting to form in the early morning, casting a blue light over the land. Bay made her way down the hall, quiet as a ghost, she was light, and her bare feet made no sound on the floor. She wore a white cotton nightgown, in her hand she clutched a tall candle, the only light in the house.

Her long blond hair was no longer in an uncomfortable bun, but left down to wave past her shoulders. Her heart beat with excitement. The house was so quiet, and dark, it felt so strange, and rather magical. Bay walked down the quiet hallway until she reached the end where the entrance to the attic lay.

She very carefully, and quietly pulled the attic door downward and climb up the ladder into the darkness of the attic. She moved across the floor, with her candle out in front of her lighting up the small room. She made her way to the far corner, there leaning against the wall lay the briefcase.

Bay came to her knees in front of it, her heart beating faster than it ever had. She placed down her candle and picked up the case in her lap. She placed her fingers on the outside pocket and peered inside. Something white caught her eye, she reached in her small white hand and gently pulled out a long notebook. The cover was leather bound, and the paper was thick and strong. She flipped through it, but all the pages were blank.

Then something else caught her eye, there was another item in the case. She pulled it out as well. It was a small, wrinkled piece of paper, the sides were black, and a small brown hole formed in the middle, as if someone had tried to burn it. But the words written on it were still whole, and she read them carefully by candle light, the same way they were written.

This small piece of paper is the only thing I have left to tell of the Lost Manuscript. I am sure my enemy's will find the paper and try to destroy it no matter how well I hide it. So I must give the information carefully.

Look in a place I love, that is myth,
The things I make. A tale that many
do not believe. Here you will find the
answer to the answer that you seek.

If you are of goo   eart   please protect the manuscript, and help me. Continue to give hope. Now I must go.

I am yours,   Brien Ink

Bay stared at the paper trying to figure out what it meant. Ink. That was the name the lady of the house hold had said when the briefcase arrived. She knew who he was, now Bay

2

knew why she did not want to open the case. Brien Ink was in danger, and the lady did not want to get involved. goo eart. That must be 'good heart', for this was where the flame had burnt a hole in the paper. Bay studied the riddle on the paper but it made no sense to her. It would make more sense if she knew who Brien Ink was, and what the Lost Manuscript was.

The lady, her name was Cornelia, she knew, but Bay would not dare ask her. If Cornelia found out that she had gone through private things she would kick Bay out of the house.

Bay put the burnt paper into the note book, picked up the candle and made her way back to the hallway.

The sun was appearing in the horizon. Bay could hear someone stirring in a bedroom. She replaced the attic door and jogged down the hallway to her bedroom.

She looked down at the leather bound note book in her hands and smiled. There was finally a mystery to behold in Bay's sad, and chambered life. Somehow Bay felt that Brien Ink would lead her to a place of imagination, and that she would find something in herself that she could finally unlock.

***

Bay did not sleep, instead she went downstairs early and prepared breakfast for the household. The smell of bacon quickly filled the air. While the meat cooked, Bay also browned the toast, and fried the eggs. Cooking was her favorite chore, while she cooked Bay pretended that this house belonged to her father, and that soon he would walk down the stairs and they would both enjoy the large breakfast together.

But her father did not come down the stairs. Instead the heavy footsteps of James entered her ears and a tall man with sandy-brown hair appeared. His brown eyes were kind, and the beginnings of a beard were forming on his face. Bay always liked James, he was the stable master, he cared for the horses, the barn, and the stables all by himself. He was eighteen years old, and Bay's best, and what sometimes seemed, her only friend. James was always the first person up and ready and Bay already had his plate of bacon and a piece of buttered toast ready for him.

"Good morning sunshine," he said, the sneaky smile forming on his face, the one that said he had a secret, one that he would never tell.

"Hi James," Bay handed him his plate. In a matter of minutes the contents were gone. James smiled at her, Bay felt herself flush, James always made her feel happy.

"Delicious as always," James stood up and gave her a warm smile, "I'll see you at lunch, sunshine." Then he was gone out the door into the early morning. Bay wished she could go with him to watch the sun rise, and see the horses, just as they were waking. She and James could saddle two horses and ride off together away from this place and find their own life, but this fantasy disappeared when Cornelia appeared in the kitchen.

Bay placed the egg, jellied toast, slice of apple, and cup of tea in front of her. Cornelia did not say anything, she was never a morning person. She nodded and started eating. One minute later Delon appeared, this was Cornelia's younger sister, they both inherited the house from their father, along with enough money to live comfortably for the rest of their lives. Delon was musical, she had the upper floor to herself, there she wrote and played music all day. Bay liked to sit on her bed and listen to the piano on dull days, Delon was a quiet person, very patient, unlike her sister who was strict, and practical.

Delon was small and frail, her light brown hair was short and her blue eyes were usually looking down at something.

The final person to enter the kitchen was Roan, his large red hair could be seen from yards away. This was Delon's fiancé, they were planned to wed next month. Bay did not care for Roan, but he was tolerable. He spent his evenings at the house with Delon, in the morning he went off to work, then returned about sunset. Bay did not know what he did, nor did she care.

Roan quickly ate breakfast, kissed Delon good-bye, then left without a word. Delon finished her breakfast then smiled at Bay.

"Do you want help with any of your instruments?" Bay asked hopefully. She loved being in Delon's room cleaning the instruments and listening to her play.

"No, you can go have fun today, it's a beautiful day, go outside." Bay beamed. But her smile froze when she saw Cornelia ready to protest.

"I need help in the gardens today," She said. Delon rolled her eyes.

"Don't start Cornelia, Bay has worked hard all week, she has earned it. You can work on your own gardens." Cornelia was a flower person, she was always tending to her flower, and vegetable gardens. And for some reason, she never liked to give Bay a day off. Delon on the other hand, seemed to take pity on her, and made sure Cornelia never worked her too hard.

Bay ran upstairs where she grabbed a book she had been reading. She also took the notebook and letter, from Brien Ink, from under her bed. Bay took these outside. The air was cool, and a small breeze blew her long blond hair. Bay dressed in pants, and let her hair down, this made her feel as free as a bird and she ran as fast as she could across the field to the stables.

The stables were warm, and dust filled the air, along with the smell of hay. James was standing by Ivory, a beautiful white horse, with a black nose, and golden mane. He gently moved a brush across her lovely white fur. James truly loved the horses. Bay simply stood there watching him brush her, it seemed so natural.

"Hello sunshine," James said without turning around, he always knew when someone was there.

"Hi James, Delon gave me the day off."

"She's a sweet lady."

"Yeah."

"Here, why don't you brush her a bit?" James handed

5

Bay the brush. She put down the books and started rubbing it across her coat. Ivory looked over at her then remained still. After the brushing, Bay took a comb and ran it through Ivory's mane and tail.

"There you go," Bay said patting her neck, "you look as beautiful as ever." James smiled. He opened the stable doors and Bay helped him move the horses out onto the field, where they could feed and run.

The two of them sat down under the shade of an apple tree. James picked off one of the apples and used his pocket knife to cut off the meat. He put one in his mouth, then cut off a piece for Bay.

"James, did you see the rider here yesterday morning?" Bay asked, she reached over and pulled the notebook onto her lap.

"Yes, he delivered a package to Cornelia," James answered casually.

"He delivered a leather briefcase, but she didn't open it, all she said was 'Ink'."

"Ink?" James repeated, he was going to take another bite of the apple, but he suddenly stopped.

"Yes, and last night..."

"You opened it," James finished, he always seemed to read her mind.

"Yes! Look what I found," Bay handed the notebook to him. James looked at it, but didn't open it.

"Brien Ink," he said softly.

"How did you know that?" Bay asked mystified. James sighed deeply.

"You should put this away, Bay, back in the suitcase." His words were solemn.

"Who is he James?" Bay asked. Her words were solid, and her curiosity was at it's highest.

"Brien is a writer," James said quietly. He stared at the notebook, and clutched it tightly, as if it would blow away. He remained silent for a long time, Bay simply watched him.

"What is the Lost Manuscript?" Bay asked, she decided

James would not say much more on Brien Ink. James hesitated before he answered.

"Brien wrote a book. He found secrets, secrets most people, shouldn't know about. Brien did research you know, he traveled all over the world, studying things, learning things. If you asked him any question he would know the answer. I remember him visiting here once in awhile when I was a boy. We would sit in the loft, and Brien would tell me stories. They sounded as if he made them up, but deep inside me I felt that somehow, they were true."

"And he wrote them all down," Bay continued.

"Yes, it's a book with all the secrets, and story's that Brien has ever found. He made notes when he traveled, and then he just put it all together."

"But, there is a note. Brien wrote a note, it was in the briefcase. "He said that his enemies would find him, or something like that." Here look." Bay opened the notebook revealing the burnt paper. James stared at it for a long time, his eyes studying the words written there. He slowly breathed in and out, Bay watched him, and they were both silent. Bay noticed James's hand were trembling.

"What's wrong?" Bay whispered. James swallowed, his voice was rough.

"Brien has enemies. People who do not want the secrets to be read, or the story's to be told." They have been chasing him for years, but Brien has still been trying to get the manuscript published. He makes copies and sends them to different people and different places. That way if he ever makes it to that place he can get to the book, or he can have the people he sent it to try and send it to an editor."

"Why can't he get it published?" Bay asked. Her heart was basking in wonder and curiosity.

"He is unsolicited. He just wrote stories, he never really tried to publish them. Brien wrote for the thrill of writing. And he wrote anything and everything, that is why he traveled the world, to find different stories."

"He told you all of this?" Bay asked.

"Most of it. I was just a child, he loved to tell me stories, and I loved to hear them," James raised his hand and pointed to the stable. "We always talked up in the loft, and sometimes in the attic. Always a quiet place, Brien was my best friend when my father worked here."

"Like you and me," Bay said cautiously.

"Just like you and me," James agreed. Bay smiled.

"Then one day Brien disappeared. He was always leaving, coming and going, but one day he left, and never came back." Bay didn't say anything, James was in a distant memory, his voice was sad. She felt sorry for him, how would it feel losing your best friend?

"What was Brien doing here? Is he related to Cornelia? Or Dolen?" Bay asked.

"Yes, they are his aunts, his father is their brother. Brien's father worked here, as the stable master. Brien lived on the farm since he was a child. He was almost eighteen when his father died. "Then my father was hired, I was about your age, fifteen." "Brien was allowed to live on the farm, but like I told you, he came and went like the wind." This is the first I've heard from him in years."

"Wow," Bay stared at the notebook that James still held in his hands.

"This was Brien's notebook, he was always writing in it, or drawing something."

"Why is it blank?" Bay asked. James frowned and opened the book, but only the thick white pages looked back at him.

"This must be a different book," James said still frowning, "I remember Brien always carried it around with him, writing things down, and doing sketches, he always had it with him. I think he even slept with it."

Bay giggled, James forced a smile. "Or at least hid it somewhere," James scratched his neck and shook his head. He closed the notebook and picked up the burnt letter, he studied it closely.

" 'The things I make,'" he mumbled reading the riddle aloud. "Brien made books, he loved books." James turned to

Bay. "He kept piles of them in his room, the books up in the attic are his."

"Where did he get them?" Bay asked.

"Everywhere, different countries, he met famous writers who would give him some." Some of those books are handwritten, and in different languages." Bays eyes widened with wonder.

"Didn't you ever read them?" James asked.

"I wanted to," Bay said, "I was scared that Cornelia would catch me with one though. She told me never to touch them or she would kick me out." James smiled a little.

"Sometimes her bark is worse than her bite," he said. James turned his attention back to the letter. " 'Something that is myth, that many do not believe,' It must be a book on mythology, or something like that," James said.

"What does he mean by, 'the answer to the answer,'?" Bay asked peering at the letter.

"The answer must be another question, that you have to find a second answer to," James said. He thought for a moment, "so that must mean that when we find the book that Brien is talking about, it will be another riddle."

"How do we find the book?" Bay asked.

"I'm not sure we should look for it," James said. Bay felt her heart begin to sink.

"But, Brien needs our help. "Look the paper is burnt, that means his enemies have found him, what if he is in trouble?"

"Brien Ink is always in trouble," James said.

"But he is your friend. He might have abandoned you here, but he is still the one who told you stories up in the loft, and made you feel better when you were sad."

"How did you know that?" James asked quietly.

"Because you do the same for me," Bay answered. James looked up into her blue eyes and smiled.

"You're right," James looked down at the letter, "'Continue to give hope,'" he whispered. James smiled and shook his head, "Brien, what are you getting me into?"

Bay smiled as well, and silently answered his question, an adventure.

Chapter Two

Bay laid on her bed staring at the window on the east wall. Moonlight filled up the dark room. Bay stared at the full moon shining out against the black sky, and small stars glittering around it. Bay's candle sat on the bedside table, still lit, though it had grown very short from the long hours. The clock beside the candle told Bay that it was five minutes until midnight, but she did not sleep, though she felt herself grow weary.

Bay sat up and leaned against her pillow. She reached under her covers and pulled out the leather bound notebook. She ran her hand over it's soft cover, and lovely pages. They were so white and strong, Bay had the great urge to write in them, write down anything and everything, for there can be so much to write, especially when you can't say them. Bay shut the book to fight the temptation, this was   Brien's notebook. And besides she had no pen to write with.

Bay pulled out Brien's letter from between the pages. She read through it over and over, trying to find a clue to the questions that ran through her mind. She looked up back out the window, she could vaguely see the trees, and rolling hills under the moonlight.

Where are you Brien Ink? Bay thought to herself staring out into the farm. She wished she could see past the farm into the world, like Brien could. Like Brien did.

It was now eleven fifty-nine. Bay pulled the covers off of her body and placed her bare feet on the floor. She tucked the book under her arm and picked up the candle. She quietly opened her door and peered into the hall, it was completely dark and all was silent. Bay left the room and walked down the hall without making a sound. She made it to the end, and went up the familiar ladder into the attic.

The small room was chilly, and as dark as night, there were no windows in this room. Bay walked across the floor and held her candle out in front of her, trying to see.

"James?" Her voice came out in a short breath, so that she could barely hear it. But the room was so quiet she was afraid to make any noise to loud.

"Bay," James gently whispered in her ear. Bay turned around, James was bare foot, and still wearing his work clothes, "I couldn't see who you were," James whispered, "I was hiding."

"That's okay," Bay said. She turned and walked up to one of the large chests. She undid the latch and opened it, inside were pillows and quilts. Bay grabbed two pillows and one of the quilts and brought them to James. They both sat on the pillows and wrapped the warm blanket around them. Bay set the candle on the floor so they could share the light. James grabbed a large stack of books and pulled it towards them.

"Look through them all," he instructed, "Sometimes titles can lie." Bay did not understand this but she grabbed a dusty book from the stack and set it in her lap. Her heart fluttered with excitement, she had always wanted to read these books, touch them, and study them. And now with James here beside her, she finally could, to solve Brien's riddle.

Bay cleaned the book, brushing off the dust and opened it. The pages were yellowing, and beginning to fall out, Bay felt hurt to see the book in such condition, she loved to read, it was the only way for her to leave the farm and enter a new world.

Delon, and James would bring her books when they had the chance. Bay would read them then put them under her bed, where she could always see them if she wished, or read them over. She had five books now, she had nearly read all of them three times each.

Bay began to read the words written in front of her, she did not mean to read it, just skip and study it a little, but her eyes saw the words and started to absorb them, like a thirsty plant.

The train was twelve cars long. The last car was the car that held the shipment of gold which was to be sent to London, from Cornwall England, in order to finance the war between England and France. Some officials feared that a master thief would somehow break into the car and steal the gold within, but all believed that this was impossible, it was after all a moving train, with a guard, and a safe locked with a combination and two keys. Yes everyone who discussed the gold at their tea parties all agreed it was impossible, for this reason Richard Calle planned out the great train heist.

Bay was immediately absorbed in the story, wondering how Richard Calle would steal the gold from a moving train. But before she could finish the chapter James stopped her and told her to continue looking.

"I want to see what happens," Bay protested.

"You can bring the book to your room and read it there," James said. He turned and went on studying the books. Bay looked down at hers, she feared Cornelia's punishment if she was caught with the book. But things were changing, Bay nodded and marked her spot, she set the book beside her for later reading, and grabbed a second one.

As the night wore on Bay added two more books to her stack to read later, but they were no closer to solving the riddle. James had found a few books on mythology, but none had the answers they were looking for.

It was almost three o'clock in the morning when James yawned and set down the book he was looking at.

"We had better get some sleep," he said, "we can look again tomorrow night." Bay nodded. They both sat for a second in silence to rest. In that one second they both heard the sound of footsteps out in the hall.

James jumped up and ran for the attic opening. Bay quickly pushed the books back in place and blew out her candle flame. James shut the door to the attic plunging them into darkness. Bay crawled carefully across the floor, and managed to get behind a pile of boxes, just as the attic door was opened once again.

Bay held her breath clutching the three books in her hands. She felt sweat starting to form on her brow, even though it was very cold. Candle light filled up the room, Bay noticed her own candle lying a few inches away from her, she very carefully reached out her hand and pulled the candle behind the boxes beside her. Even a small clue like that could give away their presence.

Footsteps softly padded across the floor. Bay turned her head and peered out from behind the boxes to see who the intruder was. Bay instantly recognized the bright red hair, it was Roan. Bay looked around the room quickly trying to find James, but he was well hidden.

Roan walked across the attic and began looking around. He opened boxes, and peered into dark corners. Bay frowned, what could he be looking for in the middle of the night? Roan walked to the other side of the room passing Bay. He came so close Bay could have touched him, but it was only for a second and he was out of range.

Roan went to the far corner and stopped. He bent down and then stood up once again, in his hand he clutched Brien's briefcase. Roan licked his lips and tucked the case under his arm. Very quickly, and quietly he walked across the room back to the opening. Bay listened to his footsteps on the ladder, then there was a creak, and thump, as the attic door closed, and the room became black once again.

Bay closed her eyes and counted to ten. She reached into her pocket pulling out a match and lit her candle. Bay sucked in air, and wondered how long she had held her breath. She stood up and came out from behind the boxes.

"James?" She whispered carefully. A loud creaking sound answered her. Bay turned around and saw James crawl out of a wooden chest. He coughed and brushed the dust off his clothes.

"Who was that?" He asked.

"It was Roan, he took Brien's case," Bay said, she felt herself grow nervous and tense.

"Why would he want that?" James mumbled to himself.

"Maybe he knows about Brien Ink," Bay suggested.

"I don't see how, he has only lived here for a few months," James said. They were silent for a moment, Bay set down her candle and quickly put the quilt and pillows away.

"I'll see if I can spy on him a bit, in the mean time just act casual. We will look through the books again tomorrow night, the same time," James said.

"All right," Bay agreed. She picked up her books and followed James to the ladder. James undid the latch and gently pushed it open. He went first then helped Bay down.

"Go on to your room, I'll sneak out the window," Bay walked down the hall, and they both slipped into her bedroom unnoticed.

Bay sighed with relief, they were safe in her bedroom. Bay locked the door and sat on the bed. She covered herself in the warm blankets and sighed with relieve.

"Good night sunshine," James whispered. He leaned forward and kissed her forehead.

"Do you miss Brien?" Bay asked.

"All the time," James said, without shame. He looked at her for a while, "you miss your dad," he said matter of factly.

"Yes," Bay answered, "It's not so bad now. Dad use to say time heals all wounds."

15

"He will come back, don't worry." James stood up and went to Bay's window. He glanced back and waved at her, then he jumped out and disappeared into the night.

Bay closed her eyes and snuggled deep into her blankets, she was too tired to think about anything, though Roan did prey on her mind a little bit, perhaps tomorrow she would figure out what he wanted with Brien's briefcase. Until then there was only a deepening darkness, as Bay fell into sleep.

***

Bay was awoken by Cornelia that next morning. Sunlight shined through her window, and a beautiful blue sky greeted her, Bay wished she could have woken up to these instead of Cornelia's glaring gaze.

"You should have been up nearly a hour ago," she scolded. Bay blinked and looked at her clock, it read eight in the morning, breakfast started at six, or seven o'clock.

"Sorry," Bay mumbled sitting up and trying to remain focused.

"You will be sorry if you can't keep up with your chores, and I kick you out of this house." You need to find a new threat, Bay shot back silently in her mind.

"Get up, I want that kitchen spotless in half a hour, and Delon needs her instruments cleaned. You stayed up late didn't you? Reading no doubt, if this happens again I'll take your books away."

If you can find them, Bay thought, and smiled to herself, pleased at her own slyness. There was a loose floor board in the room, Bay had moved her bed on top of it so that no one would step on it, but it soon proved to be an excellent hiding place. Her newly acquired books now lay safely under the board, along with a small wooden box which held a necklace her father had given her, a piece of quarts she had found at the creek by the farm, a glass perfume bottle someone had tried to throw away, and a bracelet James had given her for her birthday.

Bay yawned and sat up, Cornelia glared at her and left the room. Bay stared at the closed door with anger. She despised Cornelia so much, how dare she threaten to take her books away

16

when they were the only thing she had left? Cornelia acted like Bay wanted to be here. Bay clenched her fist, and punched her pillow pretending it was Cornelia's face.

"Do me a favor Cornelia," Bay whispered out loud as she got dressed. "Go get lost for a few days, shave your hair, let it grow back then come back home." Bay combed her hair, and brushed her teeth. She then went downstairs to the kitchen. It was a beautiful day, that meant that Cornelia would be outside in her gardens, good. Then Bay could have the house to herself.

Bay entered the kitchen, but stopped in surprise. Roan sat at the table sipping some porridge, that Delon had made. A newspaper laid beside him, but he wasn't reading it.

"What are you doing here?" Bay asked though she knew it was rude. Roan glanced up at her casually.

"I live here," he explained sarcastically. Bay narrowed her eyes at him in anger, Roan always treated her as if she were five.

"I meant, why aren't you at work?" She said gritting her teeth.

"Apparently I got the day off," he said, "So I'm staying home to work on something."

"Work on what?" Bay asked. She moved into the kitchen and picked up a dust cloth.

"That is no business of the maid is it?" Roan said purposely. Bay felt her insides turn to fire, she twisted the cloth in her hands and heard the fabric rip.

"I am not the maid," She said struggling to keep her voice down.

"You could have fooled me," Roan said teasingly.

"It's easy to fool you Roan," Bay said, she smiled to herself when she saw Roan's smirk become a frown.

"You watch yourself missy, I won't tolerate that tone." Bay spun around and glared at him. Roan was surprised at that look, if looks could kill, he thought to himself, I would be dead right now.

"Nether will I," Bay snapped, "You forget that I hate it here, and I'm not scared of losing my job."

"So why are you still here?" Roan challenged her. Bay remained silent, continuing to stare at him. "Because you have nowhere else to go," he answered for her, "So don't push it missy."

Roan stood up and left the kitchen. Bay only stood in the middle of the room staring down at the cloth in her hands. She felt tears form on her eyes, Roan was right, she had no where else to go, she was stuck here until her father came back.

Bay sighed in depression. She picked up Roan's bowl of unfinished porridge and cleaned it. She cleaned up the kitchen, deep in thought. Roan said he was working on something.

Brien's case. That must be it, why did he want it though? Bay finished the kitchen then took off her shoes. She walked out of the kitchen, and upstairs to the second floor. Roan's bedroom door handle was not closed, that meant the door was ajar.

Bay walked down the hall as quietly as possible. She paused in front of the door, unsure of snooping on Roan. There would be punishment if he saw her. But Bay knew she had to look, just for a moment. She reached out her hand and very gently pulled the door open less than an inch. She bent forward and peered through the crack.

Roan sat on his bed with his back to her. Bay tilted her head to the right and saw the corner of Brien's briefcase on his lap. Roan had opened it and was going through the pockets, Bay watched as he searched in vain for the items that the case held, she knew he would find nothing, and she smiled, glad that she and James had outsmarted him.

Bay started to close the door when a hand suddenly reached out and covered her mouth. Bay jumped, and a strong arm pulled her away from the door. Bay jerked out of her capture's grasp and spun around. James stood in front of her, Bay sighed in relief. James put a finger to his lips and took Bay's wrist. He led her down the hall and they slipped into her room.

"You scared me to death!" Bay said, she sighed once again and sat on the bed.

"You will get in trouble for doing that, I told you I would spy on Roan," James said. He sat on a rocking chair.

"Well it doesn't matter," Bay said, "Roan was looking through that briefcase, why would he want that?"

"Maybe he knows about Brien," James said, "he could have been looking for that letter, or the manuscript."

18

"Why though? Is he good or bad?" Bay asked, though she had decided to herself that Roan was not to be trusted.

"Either way we will keep an eye on him," James said, "In the mean time let's try and solve that riddle. I have an idea." Bay leaned forward eagerly, her heart felt light once again as she listened to James's plan.

The two of them went down the hall together to Delon's room. Delon was at her piano working on a new piece, her fingers ran across the keys quickly and gracefully, producing the beautiful music.

"That was very nice Miss Delon," James said.

"Thank you, it needs a bit of work though. What do you need dear?" Delon asked. Bay sat down at a chair and picked up Delon's flute, pretending to clean it.

"I just wanted to tell you that I need some knew horseshoe nails, they are beginning to rust."

"All right, I'll ask Roan to pick some up tomorrow." Bay suddenly went into a fit of coughing. She bent over letting out loud deep coughs. They subsided and Bay gasped for air, rubbing her chest.

"Are you all right?" Delon asked. She bent over and touched Bay's forehead, "you don't have a fever."

"I have been coughing like this since last night, I don't know what's wrong," Bay said.

"It's probably the attic," James put in, "when was the last time you cleaned it?"

"Well it's been awhile," Delon said thoughtfully.

"It's probably the dust from the attic ventilating through the house. You should have it cleaned before it makes everyone else sick."

"That's a good idea," Delon said.

"I'll clean it ma'am," Bay volunteered.

"Are you sure Bay? It will take you a few days, and it's awfully messy up there."

"I don't mind, really, it's no problem."

"All right, James give her a hand though. Go on you two, I have work to do," Delon waved her hands gently at them. Bay followed James out into the hall where they smiled at each other.

"That was a good fit of coughs," James said.

"Thank you. Let's get started on that attic." They walked down the hall and climbed up the ladder into the attic.

Bay lit her candle, and James pulled out more books, setting them in stacks. They sat down on the floor with their pillows and continued their search through the piles of books. Bay enjoyed every minute of it, she was swallowed up into the different worlds of the books; stories of haunted houses, fairy tales, with talking animals, sailors who hunted giant whales, and the distant future, and dark frightening places where brave men would not venture.

The hours past by, but Bay, nor James noticed or cared, they were no longer in the dark attic, they were riding winged horses, and dueling with knights. Only were they pulled out of these worlds when their names were called from below the stairs.

"Bay, James! Are you up there?" It was Delon.

"Yes Miss!" James called. They quickly stood up and pushed the books away. Bay jumped up and went to the stairs to keep Delon from coming up.

"Yes ma'am?" Bay asked.

"That's enough cleaning for today. Let's make some lunch, you must be starving." Bay and James came down into the lighted hallway. Bay wished they could read out here instead of the dark attic.

Before they entered the kitchen with Delon, James took Bay aside. "I know you slept in this morning, I don't want you to get in anymore trouble, so we will skip the night time reading, and just look in the day."

"But we'll waste valuable time," Bay protested.

"We have plenty of time. Don't worry okay? We will look again tomorrow." Bay nodded, and followed James into the kitchen where Delon was preparing some chicken for lunch. Bay helped her cook, but her mind was else where. It was back up in the attic with all those books, waiting patiently to be opened, and read. Bay knew she couldn't wait for the morning. After lunch she took a nap. She would need it for the night ahead.

Chapter Three

Once again Bay merely laid on her bed staring at the, now moonless sky. Her eyes would drop, and twice she almost dosed off, but the thought of finding Brien's book kept her awake. At half past eleven she got out of bed. She was afraid if she waited another thirty minutes she would fall asleep.

Bay lit her candle and walked carefully down the dark hall and back up to the attic. The small room, was chillier than last night. Bay found the quilt and wrapped it around herself. She found a pillow and sat down on the floor. Bay smiled as she picked up the next book in the stack she had been reading earlier that day. This was a very thick book with a black hard cover. The golden letters spelled out the title: The Poems of Edgar Allen Poe. Bay had heard of Poe, but had never read his work. With an eager heart she opened the book and began to read.

The minutes slipped by as Bay read the errie, and strange stories of Poe. When she had finished the poems, she marked the book and laid it beside her for later reading.

Bay paused before moving on to another story. It was so stuffy in the attic, and cold, she wished there was a window. That would be really nice.

Bay stood up with the quilt still wrapped around her, and her candle in hand. She walked across the cold floor to stretch her tired body. As she walked she past the east wall, and a cool breeze ruffled her nightgown. Bay turned and came to her knees to see where the breeze came from. Her candle flame flickered, and almost went out. Bay set the candle down and peered at the wall trying to figure out where the wind was. She felt the cool breeze on her face once again, there was a hole in the wood, probably caused by ancient termites. Bay closed one eye and looked through the hole. She could see a bit of the night sky, with stars doting it, glittering down at her. Bay raised her hand and picked away at the molding wood, soon a hole as big as her fist was formed. Bay put her mouth to it and breathed in the fresh night air.

She stood up and pick up her candle, deciding that she should start looking through the books again. Bay turned but as she did her foot struck something hard. Bay winced and looked down to see what she had stepped on.

A large book laid on the dusty floor, it had been hidden under a pile of dirty sheets. Bay picked it up and held the candle at a careful angle to study it. It was a large book, colored red. Someone had hand drawn a dragon on the front in ink, there was no title.

Bay sat down on the floor staring at the strange book. She opened it revealing familiar strong white paper, the same in Brien's notebook. Everything in this book was handwritten, and sketched. On the title page were the words, *Dragon Tails by Brien Ink.*

Bay's heart pounded with excitement, a book written by Brien Ink. She had longed to read one of his books, now was her chance.

Bay turned the pages carefully, absorbing each word written. This book was about dragons. Brien had written dozens of stories, and legends that he had heard from towns in Scotland, Ireland, Greenland, and England about dragons in the area. In the back he had even put down his records of searching for the dragons. Written on the very last page was this:

The Dragon's Riddle

The place where stories were told
to the young from the old.
The horses give their lovely song
    Somewhere safe, away from the wrong.
    Way up high amongst the trees.
This private riddle you will see
a strange story I give to thee.

Bay stared at the riddle. Her mouth slightly open in surprise. This is it, her gut whispered to her. Bay clutched the book tightly, she read the poem again, then again.

Was this the riddle they were searching for? James would know. Bay jumped up dropping her blanket. With the book tucked under her arm, and the candle in hand, Bay rushed across the room and climbed down the ladder. She started to run down the hall, but stopped herself and went back to shut the attic door. She then raced down the hall, her feet making soft thumps on the floor, but she did not believe anyone heard her. Bay ran downstairs, James slept in the spare room by the sitting room. Bay went into the room without knocking. James was lying on his bed, bare chest. James's room was small but he liked it that way. There was a large wooden box in the corner holding James's clothes and some personal items. A small mirror sat on top of the box. A small table and chair were in the other corner, papers were scattered over the table, with a single pen sitting on top of them.

Bay walked into the room and shook James's shoulder. He mumbled something and turned over. Bay shook him harder,

"James, wake up I found something," she whispered.

James's eyes flickered and opened. Bay shook him again so that he would not fall asleep again. "James!" Bay snapped. James eyes began to focus.

"Bay?" he mumbled, "go to sleep, it's late."

"Wake up!" Bay said forcefully. James blink a few times, "what?" he asked.

"I found something," Bay said. She placed the dragon book on James chest. James looked at it then sat up.

"There is a riddle in this book in the back. Brien Ink wrote it. It's about dragons, it fits Brien's clue in the letter. Look at it!" James took Bay's candle and studied the book carefully. He flipped through the pages, studying them carefully. He seemed more absorbed in it than Bay was.

"Look in the back," she said, "the last page." James turned the paper and read the riddle.

"What do you think?" Bay asked when he was done reading it.

"It could be it. It's mythology, Brien loved dragons, they were his favorite story lines. But this riddle doesn't make much since."

"Riddles are not suppose to make since, that's why you have to solve them," Bay said.

"You are enjoying this aren't you?" James said with a bit of a smile. This question caught her off guard, she was enjoying this, the thrill of adventure, the mystery. Just like in the stories.

Bay smiled, "does the riddle make any since to you?" James read through it again, "I'll have to think about it," he said, "here, you keep the book. Could you copy the riddle on a paper over there?"

Bay walked over to the table. She found a blank sheet amongst all the filled ones, but she could not read the papers due to James's scrawly handwriting. She copied down the riddle and let out a loud yawn.

"Go to bed sunshine, it's been a long night." Bay smiled, she rubbed her hand over the leather bound book in her hands.

The night had been long, tomorrow would be even longer. Bay left James's room and went back upstairs.

Bay walked down the hall, but a sound reached her ears, a creaking of wood. Bay slowly turned around, but she only made a ninety degree angle turn when a dark figure placed a large hand over her mouth and shoved her against the wall.

Bay's head hit the wood, she winced with pain, and made a very soft moaning noise.

"Shh," Bay immediately recognized Roan, and her stomach twisted in fear. "You don't want to wake the ladies do you?" Roan's voice was silent and evil, Bay had always disliked him, but now she was terrified of him.

"They wouldn't like the fact that you have been sneaking off at night stealing books from the attic, oh yes I know what you have been doing." Roan pushed Bay forward with his hand still clasped over her mouth, and his arm wrapped itself around her arms so that she couldn't break free. Bay clutched the dragon book in her arms tightly.

Roan moved her down the hall and shoved her into his room. Bay stumbled forward when he released her. Roan shut the door and locked it.

"What do you want?" Bay said, trying to sound brave, but she did not think her voice was convincing.

"What do you know about the suitcase the rider delivered here a few days ago? You took it up to the attic."

"What are you talking about?" Bay tried to sound confused. Roan narrowed his eyes and stepped towards her. Bay walked away from him, and felt her back hit the wall, she was trapped. Roan leaned toward her until his face was merely inches from hers, Bay kept eye contact, to show him she was not afraid. Even though she wished she could faint.

"You opened the briefcase," he said quietly, "what was in it?" Bay thought quickly.

"I did look in the briefcase, but there was nothing in it.

Why? what's going on?" Roan chuckled.

"You are a good liar Bay, I'll give you that, but I want to know what was in that briefcase, now." Bay trembled, Roan's green eyes stared into hers, she looked away from them, but she could still feel them staring at her.

Suddenly, with a jerk, the book she was holding was snatched from her grasp. Bay gasped in surprise and tried to grab it back, but Roan held it out of her reach. He balanced the book on his hand and flipped through the pages carelessly. He only became interested when he came to the last page, and read the riddle. Bay sucked in her breath.

"What does this riddle mean?" he asked Bay. She shook her head.

"I don't know. You're right, I have been taking books from the attic, that's one of them. But there wasn't anything in that briefcase, I swear."

Roan stared at her, with a snap he closed the book and held it out to her. Bay quickly took it.

"Go to bed Bay," Roan said, "It's late."

"Are you going to tell Cornelia?" Bay asked, her voice trembled with relief. Roan stared at her for a moment, then a sly smile crossed his face.

"Not tonight," he said. Roan crossed the room and opened the door. Bay took a step forward, then quickly jogged out of the room. She rushed down the hall not looking back. She rushed into her room, and locked the door.

Bay fell onto her bed trying to recover from her scare. Bay caressed her book, holding it to her chest, as if it were a new born baby. She opened it and read the riddle again, this time trying to find the answer.

The horses give their lovely song. Horses, they had horses, in the field and stable, could that be it? *The place where stories were told, to the young from the old.* Bay's memory traveled back... *"We would sit in the loft, and Brien would tell me stories..."* James had told her that. The loft was in the stables, actually above the stables. Like in the trees... *Way up high, amongst the trees.* Bay's heart began to pound, she read the

26

last part out loud, *"This private riddle you will see, a strange story I give to thee."* Bay jumped up out of her bed, she started for the door, but stopped. What if Roan was still awake? Bay sucked in her breath nervously, and let go of the door handle. There was more than one way to skin a cat.

Bay turned and opened her window. The sun was becoming visible in the distance, the comforting colors of gold, and red, and pink, and purple were started in form in the sky.

Bay looked down at the ground below. If James could escape this way, so could she. Bay hid the dragon book under her bed then crawled out onto the window sill. She rotated, and gripped the ledge with her hands, and very carefully lowered herself down as far as she could.

The cool morning air blew her hair and touched her skin, Bay didn't think about getting dressed. She glanced down, the ground was closer now, but close enough?

Bay took a deep breath and let go. She fell through the air and landed on the wet ground. She lost her balance and fell onto her back. The wet grass soaked through her gown and made her shiver from the morning cold.

Bay stood up and brushed off the grass. It felt strange on her bare feet, but in a good way. Bay smiled and started to run. The cold air rushed past her, blowing her long blond hair behind her. The warm early sun touched her skin and warmed her. Bay never felt so free, and alive. She raced across the field to the stables.

She entered the small building quietly, but the horses were already awake. They watched her calmly, with warm friendly eyes. Bay went up to Ivory and patted her soft nose, Ivory made a sighing noise and sniffed Bay's hand for food. Bay turned and walked carefully down the row of horses. Tip toeing, so as not to get a splinter in her feet. Bay came to the end of the row, where a ladder leaned against the wall. She placed her feet upon it and pulled herself upward, climbing up into the loft.

Bay had to duck her head slightly to avoid the low ceiling. The loft was covered in hay, and some of the stable tools were stored up here as well. Bay walked across the loft wondering where she should look for the manuscript. Bay studied the walls and floor. She searched through the hay, but didn't look long, that didn't seem like a good place to hide something. She looked through the tools as well, but shovels, rakes, brushes, horseshoes, and tool boxes where all she found. She looked through the tool boxes as well, but found nothing. Bay sighed with discouragement, where could you hide a book up in a loft?

Maybe it wasn't the loft, she solved the riddle wrong. That sounds like something I would do, Bay thought miserably to herself. She sat down in the hay and pulled her knees up to her chest.

She thought about the riddle, but couldn't think of what else it could mean, especially the part concerning the horses, what else could it mean but the stables? Maybe this wasn't the right book, she had solved the first riddle wrong. There must be another book up in the attic with another riddle inside it.

Or maybe there was no riddle, the whole thing was a gag, perhaps Brien Ink had made up the clue to confuse his enemies, well it was working, and not on his enemies. Bay looked up out the window on the east wall. The sun had risen higher, the top of it was now visible. Bay felt miserable, she didn't want to go inside and make breakfast, she didn't want to see Cornelia's grumpy face, and Roan's eyes staring at her. She definitely didn't want to see Roan again.

I have to get away, Bay thought. She closed her eyes, so that all she could see was darkness. I wish I could get away, but Roan was right, she had no where to go.

Bay opened her eyes, and in the corner of her left one she saw something dark. Bay spun her head around in fear, her first thought was that it was Roan, but someone she had never seen before sat cross legged on the floor in front of the ladder. He had dark hair, and dark eyes, they watched her patiently, and a small smile was on his lips. He wore a long black coat, and a brown leather bag was wrapped over his shoulder.

Bay stared at him in surprise, the man's smile widened, he

28

seemed pleased that he had been able to sneak up on her so efficiently. They only watched each other for a long while before Bay found the courage to speak.

"How long have you been there?" she asked. The first question to slip out of her mouth, she felt too nervous to think about proper questions.

"I saw you come into the stables, I thought it was rather early for a young girl to be out in the barn bare foot. I was curious so I followed you." He had a laid-back voice, it was kind and thoughtful, and deep. Bay liked it.

"You weren't sitting there the whole time," Bay protested. The man's smile got bigger.

"I watched you down below, I wanted to see the horses before I came up. You were looking at the sun rise when I came up the ladder."

"You were awful quiet," Bay said.

"I have learned to be very quiet," the man said. Bay paused for a moment.

"Why did you follow me?" she asked.

"I was just riding down the road, and I thought I would stop by," the man said casually. Bay stared at him for a long time, she was beginning to understand.

"There are a lot of memories here," The man said studying the room.

"A lot of stories?" Bay asked. The man smiled and chuckled.

"There are many of those," he agreed. "What is your name little one?"

"Bay," she said. And she wished she could say more, but that was it, just Bay. Three letters.

"Bay," the man said thoughtfully, "That is Vietnamese, it means unique." Bay widened her eyes in wonder, she had always thought Bay was like the ocean.

"How do you know?" Bay asked.

"I've been around, you learn a few languages like that." The man sat and smiled at her.

"You haven't told me your name," Bay said, but in her heart she all ready knew it.

"Brien Ink, at your service, Miss Bay." Bay felt her lips form a smile, her heart started to beat with pleasure.

"You are Brien Ink," she said.

"The one and only," Brien said.

"I know you!" Bay cried happily, "I got your letter! I was trying to find your book, the Lost Manuscript. James told me all about you!"

"James," Brien said, "I wish he could leave this place. But there is still time, of course. It's never to late for something." Brien paused for a moment, "Did Cornelia, or Delon get my letter?" Bay shook her head.

"Cornelia told me to put it up in the attic, when the briefcase was delivered. And I looked inside it." Brien shook his head sadly.

"Poor Cornelia, I pity her, I really do. She believes that the world is against her, and so she is against the world." Brien shook his head again. "What about Delon?" he asked.

"She didn't know about the case," Bay said. Brien nodded.

"She is a sweet woman, but her head is in the clouds. If she came down for awhile she would notice things she never has before."

Bay smiled with wonder over this strange man. "James and I read your letter though," She said, "we were trying to solve your clue." Brien smiled. Bay thought it was a strange smile, it was as if he knew what she had been doing up here all along.

"And what have you found?" Brien asked, his strange smile never leaving his face.

"The book you wrote, Dragon Tails." We thought that the riddle in the back of the book would lead us to your manuscript."

"And has it?"

"You tell me," Bay said, "I can't find the hiding place."

"That riddle was meant for James to solve. I wrote it for him, because I could trust him, and because he was the only one who knew about this," Brien raised his hand, and reached over his head. Above him was a small nail sticking out of the wood. Brien grabbed the nail and pulled it. The wooden board it was connected to opened up like a door, reveling a secret compartment.

Bays eyes widened with surprise, she would have never known that secret was there.

Brien stood up and dusted off his pants, "go on, take a look," he said stepping aside so that Bay could see the compartment. Bay stood up and brushed the hay off her gown. She walked across the loft to Brien, he watched her with smiling eyes. Bay bent down slightly and peered into the compartment.

There were only two things in this hole. A large notebook, and a wooden pencil. Bay reached inside and pulled out the notebook, it looked like the one that had arrived in the briefcase. Bay opened the leather bound cover, inside thick white pages stared up at her. Black printed words ran across the pages in an even flow. Written at the top of the page in lovely flowing handwriting was the title:The Lost Manuscript.

Bay smiled and ran her hand over the paper, it had been here the whole time, for years, safely kept hidden inside that secret compartment. Bay turned and gently handed the book to Brien. He took it and looked at it as if were a child that he was not sure was his.

"There has been a lot of trouble for this book," he said, "I have often thought of destroying it, but...I just don't have the heart to do so." He smiled at Bay.

"Thank you for trying to find it," He said. Bay nodded her head.

"It was my pleasure." Brien studied her for a moment, then chuckled.

"I am sure that it was. Come now you will get sick with your feet all wet." Brien held out an elbow to her, Bay began to take it when a loud voice made her jump in fear.

"Don't touch her!" Bay looked down in surprise, and saw James running up the ladder, a pocket knife clutched in his hand. James jumped onto the loft and grabbed Bay's arm. He pointed the knife at the man in front of her, but when he saw him, he froze and his mouth dropped. Brien watched him with interest. James stared at him for a long while before managing to say his name.

"Brien?" Brien smiled and winked. James dropped his hand, and a smile formed on his lips.

"Brien, where did....why?..." James seemed speechless. Brien chuckled.

"You always had a way with words my friend. And welcomes," he added nodding to the knife. James quickly lowered his hand and put it away.

"I'm sorry Brien, I though you were a stranger, with Bay," he nodded to her. Bay blushed a little.

"Most understood," Brien said smiling, "Now I suggest we go back to the house for introductions, and some breakfast. And so the young lady can get some proper clothing on, I refuse to believe that Cornelia has sunk so low as to make you wear rags." Bay giggled, and they made their way down the ladder and back across the field to the house, this time they came in the front door.

The house was empty and silent when they entered. Brien studied the kitchen, taking in the old memories. Bay quickly ran upstairs to change. She cleaned and dried her feet. She almost put on her maid dress, as she called it, but she did not want Brien to see her dressed in that. Bay instead put on pants, and riding boots, this was much better. Bay cleaned herself up, then went back to the kitchen. Brien had all ready started breakfast, bacon was sizzling on a skillet and eggs were slowly becoming white.

"You don't have to help," Bay said.

"I find that as a guest it is always good to make yourself useful, especially when you are uninvited." Bay smiled.

"Why were you out in the stables Bay?" James asked, sitting down at the table. "The riddle," Bay explained, "in the dragon book, I solved it. Then Brien came and showed me the secret compartment in the loft." James shook his head.

"I should have known, it makes since now. But I was half asleep at the time. Can I see the manuscript?" Brien reached into his brown leather bag and handed James the book. James studied it and flipped through the pages with great interest. Then a sadness came over his eyes, and he shut it.

"Why are you doing this Brien?" Brien paused over the bacon, he looked at James, but not in confusion.

"You are risking your life, and your friends lives, over this," James held the book in the air, for all to see.

"You wouldn't understand James, I'm a writer. This," he pointed at the book, "is what I do, it's me, it's my life."

"It's a book," James said, anger was creeping into his voice.

"It's more than a book," Brien said. There was only patience, and sadness in his voice, "I can't explain it any better, James," Brien said. "I love writing," he whispered, James didn't hear him, but Bay did.

"Why do you have enemies who want the book Brien?" Bay asked. Brien gave her a half smile.

"The stories in that book came from all over the world. There are legends from small villages, murders in the large towns, but not regular murders that you read in the paper, these are killings that police don't want people to know about. There is a story on how a woman was saved from lava flow from a volcano by a man whom she claimed could fly. I once went to a town who claimed there was a house there, haunted by kind, and desperate spirits. I spent the night in that house." Bay's mouth dropped in fear and her eyes widened with wonder.

"Were there really ghost there?" she asked. Brien did not smile, he turned his head, and Bay noticed a white streak in his dark hair, at the temple. Her eyes became wider.

"I wouldn't take that 'old wives tale' to lightly," he said. Bay nodded.

"Some of the stories were told around a fire, some I found in diaries, the diary of a crazed murderer, the diary of a young boy who was locked in a windowless room for almost two months, and the diary of a man who was lost in the Himalayan mountains for a week. Records from survivors who crossed the Bermuda Triangle, magical birds who will grant wishes, talking animals, and people about three feet tall," Brien shook his head and laughed, "I could play riddles with them all day, they are very clever."

"But Brien," Bay cut in, "these sound wonderful, why would people want to stop you from publishing it?" Brien looked sad again.

"Some of the mysteries I solved, that police couldn't, and murders I wrote about, well lets just say that some people want to keep their secrets buried. That's why I hid the manuscripts, in familiar, and unfamiliar places so that I can run from my enemies, but continue to send my books to editors. Actually, there are only two copies of the manuscript left."

Bay gasped in horror, "where is the second copy?" Brien gave her a sly smile.

"Some secrets, I get to keep," he said. Bay felt disappointed, but she didn't push the question.

"Are you going to send this one to a publisher?" Bay asked.

"As soon as I can. There is a company in England I will try, but first I need to make some more copies of the book. I just slipped past Rivan in London, so I need to lie low for a couple of days as well."

"Who is Rivan?" Bay asked.

"Rivan is my arch enemy, you might say, or at least my most powerful, his story is the one I am most anxious about telling the world, a very interesting and dark one at that. He is also the most desperate at catching me. He is a very esoteric fellow."

"He was chasing you in France?" Bay asked, she became so interested in Brien's story that she had forgotten her eggs. James had stood up and was flipping them over for her.

"Yes, I was trying to contact an editor there. But Rivan found me, so I sent my letter to the closes relation possible, Whipshire England, home of Cornelia, and Dolen, and my old friend James Bonding. I had already left a manuscript and a riddle there, so I sent a letter with a clue to the riddle, hoping

34

someone would find it and keep it safe."

"Why was there a blank notebook in your briefcase?" Bay asked.

"My notebook? I figured that was where it was. I carry that briefcase around with me, I forgot the notebook was in there." Brien spun around and took a plate from the cabinet, he placed the cooked bacon on the plate and placed it on the table. Bay finally remembered her eggs and set them out as well. She then browned the toast and they sat down to the table.

They had barely started eating however, when Cornelia entered the room. Bay could only feel fear as the tall woman came in and saw Brien. When she did she gasped and stumbled backwards, clutching her chest. Brien stood up quickly and took her hand, but Cornelia pulled away.

"What are you doing here?" She snapped, trying to redeem herself. Brien smiled pleasantly, and gave a small bow.

"I just came to visit my favorite aunts," he said.

"Aunts?" Bay looked at James who nodded.

"Brien's father was Cornelia's brother. They all lived and worked in this house," he explained, "I told you that." Bay remembered that he had.

"A lot of good he did you too," Cornelia said glaring at Brien, "always letting you run around wild, no discipline, or control." Cornelia shook her head, "I guess it was because of your mother, he always wanted you to be happy after her death, I'll give him that, but there is a fine line between being happy, and being spoiled."

Brien only smiled, "It really is good to see you again Cornelia, I have missed your lovely face, and charming personality." Bay covered her mouth trying to hold back her laughter, Brien winked at her.

"I suppose you are here for that book of yours?" Cornelia said, "I know you hid one here. But I will have nothing to do with it Brien, I left your package untouched, the briefcase you sent us. I'm sorry, I just cannot take a part in this."

"I understand perfectly aunt Corny..."

"Don't you dare call me that!" Bay ducked under the table, trying to stifle her laughter. James too was chuckling to himself.

"Very sorry, Cornelia, old habits die hard. Anyway, I have all ready gotten the manuscript."

"Good, then you can go." Brien's face now became serious. He placed his hand gently on Cornelia's shoulder and turned her away from Bay and James. Bay quietly stood from her chair, and sneaked up on them to hear what they were saying.

"Cornelia, Rivan is back. I lost him in France, but he may be on my tail. I just need to lay low here until Lex comes back. He is a friend of mine, and he's quick. Two or three days, that's all I need. I can pay you as well."

"It's not about money Brien," Cornelia broke in, "it's the danger you put us in. What if Rivan comes here? I have a little girl to take care of. And James is a courageous boy, he would get hurt."

"I wouldn't let anything happen to them," Brien said. His voice sounded so deep and serious, it frightened Bay.

"I know you wouldn't," Cornelia actually sounded kind, it was a side of her Bay had never seen. Cornelia touched Brien's cheek. "You are still family," she said. Brien kissed her cheek. Bay quickly sneaked back to her chair, and sat down, just as they turned.

"We have a whole selection here for you this morning," Brien had returned to his casual self, "what would you like for breakfast?"

"A strong cup of tea to start with," Cornelia said sitting at the table, with a loud yawn, "and Brien," Cornelia grabbed Brien's shirt and whispered something in his ear. Brien laughed and walked to the oven to start the tea. Bay watched him out of the corner of her eye. As Brien poured the tea into the cup he slipped in a few drops of brandy. Bay's eyes widened in surprise. She had no idea Cornelia was a drinker, she decided that she would discover a lot of secrets before the week was out.

Delon appeared in the kitchen doorway at that time. But her reaction was a little better than Cornelia's.

"Brien! When did you get here? Cornelia you should have told me!"

"I only just found out myself," Cornelia mumbled drinking from her tea cup.

"It's good to see you again Delon," Brien smiled and gave her a hug. Delon hugged him back and kissed his cheek.

"Oh, it's good to see you again. I've missed you and that annoying typewriter up in the attic," Delon teased sitting down at the table.

"And I have missed that piano of yours," Brien said. He sat down at the head of the table. Bay felt a strange happy sensation, like she was sitting with a family. A strange family, but it was the closes thing she ever had. But it was about to be put on hold, Roan suddenly walked into the room.

He stared at the five people sitting at the table in confusion. He stared at Brien for a long time. Bay felt fear grip her heart when she saw him, the memory of last night haunted her.

"Who is he?" Roan asked not taking his eyes off Brien. Bay wanted to give a false name, and a false past, but Delon answered before she could.

"This is Brien Ink. Brien this is my fiancé Roan. Brien is my nephew he has come to visit us."

"You never told me about him," Roan said. He took a seat at the table, he continued to stare at Brien. Bay wished he would stop.

"Sorry Roan, I haven't heard from Brien in years, but he is here now, so you can learn all about him," Delon laughed, "that is if he will tell you."

"Brien has secrets does he?" Roan asked staring at Brien. Brien stared right back, unafraid of him. Bay wished she could have his courage.

"Everyone has secrets Roan," Brien answered, "what are yours?" Roan smiled.

"Well if I told you it..."

"Wouldn't be a secret," they both finished together. Roan chuckled.

"So what do you do Brien?" Roan asked putting some egg

in his mouth. Brien glared down at his bacon. But then he blinked, and his face was calm.

"I'm a writer," he said. Roan nodded.

"I don't think I have heard of your work," Roan said.

"I am unsolicited," Brien said, "but I'm still working on it."

"Well I wish you good luck," Roan said. Brien smirked. Bay stared at them in confusion, their entire conversation sounded sarcastic, like an act. What was going on?

Bay ate her breakfast in silence. Brien had a small conversation with Cornelia, and Delon, but beside that, not much was said. Bay kept glancing nervously at Roan, but his eyes remained on his food, and occasionally glanced at Brien.

Roan was the first to finish his breakfast, he stood up and kissed Delon's cheek. "I may be a little late tonight dear, you know they like to put extra work on you when you take a day off."

"Well, just don't stay too late," Delon said, giving him a kiss. Roan nodded to the table then left with only the snap of the door as his cue of exit.

Brien hummed a small tune as he finished his breakfast and cleared the table. He quickly stacked and washed the dishes. Bay came up beside him to dry. James put them away.

"You should come up to my room later Brien," Delon said, "I have something for you." Brien nodded and Delon left the kitchen, soon the faint sound of piano music drifted from upstairs into their ears. Cornelia finished last and stood up.

"If you need me I shall be out in the greenhouse," she informed them.

"Ah, the forbidden greenhouse, brings back memories doesn't it?" Brien asked her with the sly smile returning to his lips. Cornelia pointed a threatening finger at him, "The rules are still the same, and you stay away from my herbs." Brien laughed.

"I wouldn't dream of it," he promised. Cornelia rolled her eyes and left the house. The three of them quickly finished the dishes.

"I have to go to the stables," James informed them, "you are welcomed to join me."

"Do you still have Midnight?" Brien asked. Midnight, Bay

remembered was the oldest horse on the Hinten farm. He was completely black except for a white spot on his nose, and chest. He was very gentle, James once told her that he was the best horse to learn how to ride on because he was so patient.

James smiled, "of course we do, you know I would never let Cornelia get rid of that horse."

"Why not?" Bay asked. The three of them left the house and began the journey across the field to the stables.

"Midnight was mine when I came to live here," Brien explained, "he was a very good horse, and a friend. And he saved James's life. It was in December, James told me he was going out to the lake, and when he didn't come back, I jumped on Midnight and rode him to the lake, it was the fastest horse ride I ever had, and will ever have I'm sure. If Midnight didn't ride so fast to the lake and back James would have frozen. I found him lying by the pond, soaking wet, he had fell through the ice, and crawled back to shore."

"Wow, James you never told me that," Bay said. James simply shrugged. They entered the stables. Sunlight poured through the doorway, making the building warm up. All the horses were awake and waiting eagerly for James to let them out.

Brien walked up to Midnight and patted his soft nose, "Hey old friend, remember me?" Brien asked stroking his mussel, "mind if I take him for a quick run?" Brien asked looking at James. James smiled and shook his head.

"You ride him all day Brien, that horse has missed you." Brien smiled and began to saddle him.

"How about you Miss Bay? Would you join me in a morning ride?" Bay beamed and nodded. She turned and went to Ivory's pen. She lead the horse out and saddled her. Bay mounted and followed Brien out the stable door into the field.

"How good of a rider are you?" Brien asked.

"Let's find out," Bay said. She clicked her tongue and gently kicked Ivory forward. The white horse gallop through the field, Brien quickly followed.

Bay loved to ride the horses, she felt so free and confident. The fresh wind blew through her hair, and the sun warmed her skin.

She watched Brien, he was also a great rider, Midnight seemed to be able to read his thoughts, instead of Brien steering him. They rode on side by side through the field, Bay laughed with joy.

Brien slowed his horse, and Bay followed suit, "better give them a breather," Brien said patting Midnight's neck. They slowly walked forward back to the stables.

"You are a good rider," Brien said.

"Thanks, you are too."

"I have learned the best secrets to riding a horse, especially if you are being pursued by someone."

"Do you ever get tired of running? You know, from Rivan?" Bay asked.

"Everyday I am. Everyday I ask myself, is it worth it? And everyday the answer is the same, it is if you want it badly enough."

"Do you want it, badly enough?" Bay asked. Brien gave her a small smile.

"I'm here aren't I?" Bay nodded. "You know my story Bay, what is yours?" Brien asked. Bay paused bringing in the memories which she usually avoided.

"My father works as a delivery man for a successful company. But sometimes he has to leave the country to make deliveries, when he does, he drops me off here. I do odd jobs around the house in exchange for room and board until my father comes back."

"Then what happens?" Brien asked.

"We go home to our house across town. It's just a small out-of-the-way farm with fifty acres. Dad and I work on the farm there until he gets another delivery job."

"You don't like it here," Brien said, it wasn't a question. Bay shook her head.

"I hate it here. I think James is the only thing that keeps me from running back home every time dad leaves me here," She sighed deeply, "But even that line is starting to wear thin."

Brien looked at her sadly, "Do you know when your father is coming back?"

"I never really know, he should be back in a few days though. We usually have a guess at when he will be back, but, you know, things happen." Brien nodded.

"Look on the bright side, at least your father does return. My father died when I was seventeen."

"I'm sorry," Bay said, "Do you mind if I ask how?" She asked carefully.

Brien nodded, "It's okay. He had a heart attack, he was working with the horses." Brien smiled a little, "at least he was doing something he liked, he loved working with the horses."

"Did you like being here?" Bay asked.

"It had it's ups and downs. I lived here all my life, but there were memories of my dad everywhere. I guess that was one of the reasons I left to see the world, story ideas, and I guess I was the eager young boy ready to leave the small town."

Bay nodded in understanding, "I wish I could leave sometimes," she said.

Brien smiled, "You'll get your chance," he said, "trust me." They rode onto the stables in silence. James was cleaning out the stables when they got back. Bay and Brien unsaddled their horses, and put them out to the field. Brien gabbed a shovel and helped James clean out the stables, while Bay laid out fresh hay. The job was soon done, and they went back to the house where Bay made lemonade.

Not a lot of talking was done the rest of the day, everyone only wanted to work. The three of them spent the rest of the day cleaning the house, and helping Delon polish her instruments. At nightfall they put the horses back in the stables, and brushed them down.

Bay felt worn down by the end of the day, but in a good way. After supper she struggled to stay awake in the sitting room while Brien read and James dosed off on the couch. Bay read as well, she had brought down a book from the attic. She was no longer afraid of being in trouble for this. Somehow with Brien around she felt braver, and stronger.

Bay yawned and tried to concentrate on her book, but the words seemed to blur. Soon she could not fight it, her eyes dropped and she slipped forward in her chair into sleep.

Bay's eyes flickered open, she was being carried down the hall, she looked up and saw Brien's kind face, he smiled at her.

"Go back to sleep sweetheart, I've got you." Bay closed her eyes once again, and fell asleep. Safe in Brien's arms.

Chapter Four

Bay open her eyes, she was lying in her bed, but a strange noise had awoken her. Someone was awake and moving around somewhere in the house.

Bay sat up in bed and listened hard, voices traveled into her room, but she couldn't tell what they were saying. She pushed the blankets off of her body and went to the door. She placed her ear to the wood but could hear nothing. She carefully opened the door a crack and peered into the hallway, it was dark except for the bit of light shining through the cracks of Brien's door, next to hers. Bay felt her stomach turn in fear, who was in that room with him?

Bay stepped towards the door an put her ear to it, she could now make out the voices on the other side.

"Where is the manuscript?" a voice asked. Bay shivered when she heard it. The voice was like a piece of ice running down your spine.

"Come now Rivan, you know I won't tell you that. I thought we knew each other better," this was Brien, his voice was calm, and sarcastic, but this only made Bay feel worse. Rivan was in there.

"I had to ask," Rivan said, "I thought that after all these years you might see reason, and I am willing to show it to you. Give me all the manuscripts left, all of them, and you will never hear from me again. No more running, you can continue writing and I can go on with my life. Come now Brien you have always been a reasonable man in most circles, what do you say?"

"I can't Rivan, I can't just give up my book to you, heaven knows how you would treat it." Rivan's voice was no longer cheerfully sarcastic, it came out seriously hard.

"This is your last chance Ink, you are trapped in this house, no way out. I can just snap my fingers and there will be a hostage standing beside me, perhaps that little girl in the next room." There was a pause, Bay wished she could see their face expressions.

"You won't be touching anybody in this house," Brien said coldly.

"Only if I have to leave this room," Rivan said, "search the place!" he commanded. Bay heard large footsteps moving through the room. How many people were in there? Bay listened for a long time, but she could only hear the footsteps of Rivan's men. Finally a voice announced, "we've got it." Bay's heart sank in fear. There was silence on the other side of the door, then Rivan said, "burn it." Bay gasped. If they burned the book, there would only be one copy left.

In panic, Bay placed her hand on the door knob, she didn't know how she could stop them, maybe if she just formed a distraction that would be enough for Brien to run away. Bay started to turn the handle, but suddenly an arm wrapped itself around her arms, and a large hand pressed itself over her mouth. For a moment Bay thought it was James, but this man was much taller, and he smelled of cigarettes. Bay struggled, trying to break free of her captor, but the man was very strong, he easily pulled her back into her bedroom.

"-Rien!" Bay tried to scream out Brien's name, but the hand muffled her cries.

"Hush! Bay it's me," the man let her go and spun her

around. Bay's mouth dropped as she stared up at the tall figure. He had sharp blue eyes, and long dark hair pulled into a pony tail.

"Dad!" Bay wrapped her arms around his waist, her father hugged her back tightly, and ran his fingers through her hair.

"I'm back, it's all right."

"Dad, we have to help. There are men in the other room, they have Brien, a friend of mine. We need to call the police!"

"Bay stop, you need to be quiet. I know who those men are. But you need to tell me everything that has happened after I delivered the briefcase here."

"You delivered the briefcase?" Bay asked in confusion.

"I will explain everything, I promise. But you have to tell me what has happened, and get dressed right now, please?" Bay nodded and told the story. In the other room Brien watched solemnly as one of the two men Rivan had brought with him, held a match to his story burning away the paper.

"Where are the other copies?" Rivan asked. He sat on a chair opposite of Brien, who sat on the bed, with his hands bonded behind him. He remained silent. Rivan stood up with impatience, he was a very tall man, his brown hair was cut so short he was almost bald, and he wore a pair of black combat boots.

"I'm not playing games anymore Brien." Rivan reached into his jacket and pulled out a handgun. He pointed it at Brien's head. The writer didn't flinch, he continued to stare Rivan in the eye.

"Where are the other copies?" his voice was deep and threatening. Brien felt the same cold chill Bay had, but he did not falter.

"You will never find them if you kill me," Brien said.

"I know that," Rivan said. He pointed the gun into the air and fired a shot into the ceiling. The sound rang in their ears, and echoed through the house. Pieces of wood fell to the ground, and Rivan gave Brien an evil smile.

"Who do you think will respond to the gunshot first?" he asked. Brien could only glare at him, but behind his back his wrist were rotating slowly, as Brien applied the knowledge he had learned from an escape artist in Italy.

In the other room Bay and her father both heard the shot fired. Bay gasped in horror and went for the door, but her father grabbed her arm and pulled her back.

"We have to help! They shot Brien!"

"Hush! They didn't shoot anybody, they need Brien to find the other book copies, you will only get in trouble if you go in there. Now quick, tell me the rest, hurry." Bay briefly told him what happened after she found Brien in the stable loft. Her father nodded in understanding.

"All right Bay listen carefully. First I want you to pack some clothes, that's it, then I want you to go downstairs and get your friend James. He is with Cornelia, and Delon in his room, I told them to hide there. Take them outside, there will be a carriage there. Wait for us. When I run outside I will wave a red handkerchief at you, if you don't see a handkerchief ride off without us, and don't stop. James will take you to our house, do you understand?"

Bay nodded, she felt she might be sick with fear, but she forced it away, trying to be brave. She grabbed a bag from her closet, and put some clothing inside it. But she couldn't leave her books, she got under her bed and pulled out the dragon book, Brien's notebook, the train heist book, and her wooden box. She then pulled on her jacket, and threw the bag over her shoulder. Her father nodded and went to the door, he opened it carefully and looked into the hallway.

"All right," he said, "go, and be as quiet as possible." Bay walked out into the hall with her father behind her. He stopped by Brien's door, he reached into his long trench coat and pulled out a weapon of some kind. It looked like a sword, but it was round shape, with a blunt end, and a grip for your hands. It looked more like a golf putter without the club, more than anything. He raised it into the air, ready to strike whatever came out of the door.

Bay crept down the hall, glanced back at her father, then made her way down the stairs into the sitting room. She walked up to James's door and quietly knocked.

"James? It's me, Bay." The door was opened. James stood there fully dressed. He grabbed Bay's arm and pulled her in. Delon, and Cornelia sat on his bed looking terrified.

"Thank God you're all right," James said.

"I'm fine. Listen there is a carriage outside, my dad told us to go out there and wait for him, and Brien."

"Why is your dad here?" James asked.

"I don't know, we just have to go." James nodded. He took Delon, and Cornelia's hands and led them to the door. Bay opened it and made sure the coast was clear. The room was dark and quiet, she motioned for the others to follow her.

They sneaked out into the sitting room. Bay looked up at the stairs, she felt the urge to go back and help her father and Brien, but she had to help James and the ladies first. They walked across the room into the kitchen, then out the front door into the night.

The night air was cold on Bay's skin, she pulled her jacket on tighter. James had grabbed a lantern from the kitchen, he held it out in front of him. The road was only a few yards away, she soon spotted the carriage, with two horses ready to pull it.

James jumped up into the drivers seat. Cornelia and Delon got into the carriage, but Bay talked to James.

"My father will be waving a red handkerchief when they come out, he said that if there wasn't one to ride off to my house across town, all right?" James nodded. Bay turned her head and looked up at the house in worry.

"They will be all right," James reassured her, "trust me." Bay could only sigh, and watch the door to the house. James also watched it, and gripped the reins tightly.

***

Bay's father stood as still as a statue, with his weapon held firmly in hand. This was something he had invented

47

himself. He had gotten the metal from an old cane he use to carry after he hurt his leg. When his leg got better he found that it made a great weapon that wasn't lethal, unless he wanted it to be. He had added a grip handle to it, and had even made a special pocket for it inside his trench coat. He didn't know what it was called, to him it was simply a cane.

He had been standing next to the door since Bay left, listening to the conversation. At first there had only been silence, then Brien spoke.

"I am afraid that no one is coming to my rescue Rivan, what do you purpose to do?" There was silence for a moment, but inside the room, Rivan was giving Brien a smirk.

"I thought we knew each other better than that Brien. I always have a plan." Rivan stood up, and grabbed Brien's arm. He lifted him off the bed, but Brien had a plan as well.

He had freed his hands. When Rivan grabbed his arm, Brien pulled back his fist and struck Rivan in the face. Rivan stumbled back and Brien made a break for a door, Rivan's men ran after him.

Brien opened the door and jumped onto the floor ducking the cane. The cane came into the first man's face. His nose broke and blood fell from it. He fell to the floor, and Brien grabbed his shirt. Brien pulled the man forward and punched his face knocking him unconscious. The second man had been struck in the stomach by Bay's father, then knocked over the head.

"Lex!" Brien stood up and grabbed his arm, "I was afraid you wouldn't show up!"

"I have never let you down, Brien," Lex said. Rivan suddenly appeared behind him, and held the gun to his temple. A pleased smile was on his face.

"Get out of here Brien," Lex said. He threw his cane at him, Brien caught it, "make sure Bay protects herself."

"You better have all the copies of the manuscripts here tomorrow," Rivan said. He pressed the gun harder to Lex's head and gripped his arm. Lex quickly pulled out a red handkerchief and threw it to Brien.

"Run Brien. Take care of Bay." Brien glared at Rivan and

pointed Lex's cane at him.

"I'm coming for you," he said gravely.

"I look forward to it," Rivan said. Brien looked at Lex, and began to back away.

"Don't worry Lex, I'll be back." Lex waved his hands at him.

"Go!" Brien turned and jogged down the stairs with a heavy heart. He hated leaving Lex behind, he was his best friend. But he had to help the others, it was, after all, his fault they were in this mess.

Brien ran out the house waving the handkerchief in the air. It was very dark, Brien used the carriage lantern to guide him. He ran as fast as he could. Bay and James were sitting in the driving seat, Cornelia, and Delon were in the carriage. Brien jumped onto the driving seat next to Bay. James immediately snapped the reins and the horses took off.

"Where's my father?" Bay cried to Brien.

"Rivan has him, Bay I'm sorry..."

"No!" Bay screamed and tried to jump off the carriage, but Brien grabbed her and held her against his chest in a hug.

"Don't Bay, don't do it," he whispered in her ear, "we will get him back, I will get him back, I promise. Do you believe me?" Bay was sobbing and had her head against Brien's chest, but she managed to nod. Brien held her, and rocked her, trying to give her some comfort. But Bay could only cry. Large tears ran down her cheeks, they stained her face, and sobs escaped her mouth.

Bay laid her head on Brien's chest, listening to his heart beat. She pretended it was the only sound on earth. The noise of carriage wheels on the dirt road vanished, the horse hooves striking the ground disappeared. It was just Bay, with Briens heart beat in her ears, nothing more.

Chapter Five

Bay opened her eyes. She recognized where they were right away. It was the small white house on fifty acres, her home. She had finally dosed, as a state of defense, on Brien's chest. James stopped the horses in front of the house. Brien helped Bay down, and James led the two women out of the carriage.

"How many bedrooms do you have?" James asked.

"Four upstairs, but only two of the rooms have beds," Bay mumbled, she could care less where they slept.

"That's okay, we can roll out blankets, come on everyone." They walked up the porch to the front door. Bay pulled out the keys, and let them in. They entered a living room, the next door was a kitchen, from there were two flights of stairs, one to the second floor, and one to the basement. They all walked tiredly up the stairs to the bedrooms.

"Cornelia, and Delon can have my room," Bay said.

"James and I will sleep in the spare bedroom, you stay in your father's," Brien finished, Bay was too tired to argue. Cornelia and Delon went to Bay's room without a word. James went with them to fined extra blankets. Brien took Bay's arm and led her to Lex's room.

It was a normally spaced room, with a large bed, dresser, desk, and bookshelf. Bay put her bag on the floor and sat down on the bed, Brien sat next to her.

"I'm sorry Bay, it was my fault. I promise I will get your father back." Brien reached into his coat and pulled out Lex's cane. He handed it to Bay.

"He told me to give you this, so you could protect yourself," he said. Bay fingered the shiny metal, and handle, it fit her hands nicely. Bay gripped it hard, and suddenly had and urge to strike something with it, and pretend it was Rivan's face. But this past and Bay sighed.

"Why would Rivan take my father?" Bay asked.

"As a hostage, so that I would give up my books," Brien said.

"How do you know him?"

"We met in Romania," Brien said, "You were just a baby. I was sitting on a bridge, getting fresh air. Your father was sitting a little ways away from me having lunch. I wasn't really paying attention to him, but I heard a scream, and I saw Lex falling, and he landed in the water. I jumped in after him, and fished him out. He said I had saved his life, and was in my debt. I told him to go home but," Brien paused here, thinking back on that memory, "something just clicked, and we were friends from there on out.

"When your mother died, you were about two, I believe. Your father was a broken man, he drank when ever he got the chance, and even if he didn't. I pulled him out of a bar one night, dunked his head into the lake, and I told him, 'you are not done yet Lex. Bay needs you, and you will never pay me back by killing yourself.' I never talked about Lex's debt to me, but I said it then, and I guess something worked, because he stopped drinking, took a few weeks off work, and then things went back to normal.

"Lex was a delivery man, and someone I could trust. He

helped me run from Rivan, and would personally deliver my book to publishing houses, and bring the rejection notes back to me. But when those rejection notes came, it's like someone stabs you in the heart every time you open that envelope so hopefully, and it turns out the be the same old excuse. But Lex was always there to patch the wounds, and keep me from giving up on it. He is a true friend."

"And a wonderful father," Brien added looking at Bay, she looked back at him with sorrowful eyes.

"He loves you so much Bay, never forget that. He was just trying to keep you safe, so was I. But neither of us knew about Roan."

"Roan?" Bay asked.

"He works for Rivan, I recognized him yesterday morning. When he left for work he sent a telegram to Rivan telling him we were here, Lex managed to get here early though."

"That's why Roan was looking for your briefcase, he was trying to find the manuscript," Bay said, Brien nodded.

"Do you still have my blank notebook?" Brien asked. Bay nodded. "Don't lose it, keep it safe."

"It's one of the manuscripts isn't it?" Bay said, Brien smiled at her.

"You are unique," he said, "I used an invisible ink to write it." Bay forced a small smile. Brien touched her cheek.

"It's late, try to get some sleep little one." Brien stood up and stretched. Bay yawned, she felt to tired to do anything, but when Brien left, she put on pajamas and crawled under the covers. She smelled them, it smelled like her father. Bay pulled the blankets up to her chin and huddled in their warmth, sleep almost over took her, but then the door opened, and James came in.

"Hey sunshine," he whispered, "are you okay?"

"Better," Bay said.

"Don't worry, we will get your father back," James said. He sat down on her bed and yawned.

"Go to bed James, it's been a long day, and night. We will need our strength for tomorrow." James nodded. He kissed her forehead and stood up.

"Sleep well."

"You too." James closed the door putting the room in darkness. Bay closed her eyes and went into a fitful sleep.

Bay began to dream, and that dream turned into a nightmare. She was running across the field back at the Hinten Farm, trying to get to the stables. Rivan was behind her, trying to hit her with her father's cane. Bay's legs were like lead, weighing her down, but Bay continued to run as fast as she could to the stables, with Rivan right behind her. She could hear the cane whipping through the air. Bay ran to the stable door, and tried to shut it on Rivan, but he grabbed the door and pushed it, causing Bay to fall to the floor. She had never seen Rivan before, all she saw was a shadow, but she knew it was him.

Bay got to her feet, she turned to run, but Roan was now in front of her. He was holding Brien's notebook. and a torch.

"Don't burn it!" Bay cried, "it's Brien's last manuscript!" Roan laugh, and held the book to the flame which began to eat at it, burning away the precious paper. Bay ran forward to stop him, but he dropped the burning book, and grabbed Bay's shirt, and lifted her up into the air as if she were a bag of potatoes. Bay started to scream in fear...

Bay's eyes opened, she was gasping for breath, as if she really had been screaming. Bay sighed with relief, that was the thing about nightmares, they are just dreams, they couldn't hurt you.

Bay looked at her watch, it was past nine o'clock. Bay felt better, and rested. Clouds covered the sky outside her window, threatening rain. Bay got dressed, combed her hair, and brushed her teeth. When she was done she picked up the cane and studied it carefully, it would make a good weapon. Bay found a piece of cord and tied it to her belt, she then slipped the cane through the cord, and the cane handle kept it from sliding through. It was just like a sword scabbard. Bay put on her jacket covering the cane, and went downstairs.

Brien was all ready awake, he had brewed some coffee, made toast, and had cut up some apples. Bay and her father grew apple trees behind the house and sold them to interested buyers to make extra money.

Bay sat at the table and forced a smile to Brien, who smiled back. "Did you sleep all right?" He asked.

"Yes, surprisingly well," Bay said. She sniffed the air, it smelled of coffee beans, it was nice. "Can I have some?" Bay asked. Brien smiled and nodded. He found a mug, he poured in milk, and sugar, then just a little coffee. Bay rolled her eyes and drank it anyway, it wasn't too bad. She buttered some toast as well.

James came down next. He got a real cup of coffee, and half an apple. Delon, and Cornelia came down next. Bay noticed that Brien had sneaked a few drops of brandy in their coffee.

They ate quietly, and quickly. Afterwards Bay led Cornelia and Delon to the living room. "There are books you can read," Bay said, "Delon there is a piano in my father's study," Bay showed her the door in the living room, that led to the study. "And Cornelia, our apple tees are out back, and there are some Morning Glories growing on the fence, if you want to do some gardening."

"Thank you Bay," Cornelia said, "we will be fine." Bay nodded.

"I'll go check on James and Brien," Bay said. She went into the kitchen. Brien and James were sitting at the table in deep conversation. "What's going on?" Bay asked.

"I need to be truthful Bay, I think Rivan will kill your father even if I do give him all the manuscripts, so we need a plan."

"And what is that?" Bay asked sitting down.

"We are still thinking about that," Brien said.

"I don't think you should come Bay," James said.

"Why not?" Bay demanded, "I know I'm only fifteen, but it's still my father, I can help." James began to shake his head but Brien cut in.

"Actually she can help," Brien said, "for the first step of the plan anyway."

"Then I will," Bay said. "What is it?"

"There is a window in the attic," Brien said. Bay interrupted him.

"There is no window," She said. Brien shook his head.

"There use to be one, but, they had the glass removed and boarded over it." Bay's memory went back to the hole she had found in the attic.

"When we get to the house, James and I will go inside to make the trade, but you have a different mission...."

***

Half an hour later James, Brien, and Bay were riding in the carriage to the Hinten Farm. Bay felt scared to death, but she didn't let it show. The farm showed up quicker than Bay would have liked. Her stomach was doing back flips, and twisting itself into knots. She could only finger the cane at her waist and stare out the window. Brien and James were in the drivers seat.

The carriage moved onto the driveway, then stopped. Bay looked through the curtains of the carriage and watched James and Brien walk up to the front door. Brien had told her to wait in the carriage until they were inside, in case someone was watching them. Brien held the invisible ink copy of the Lost Manuscript in his hand, the last copy. He had warmed the pages, making the letters visible that morning.

The two men walked up to the door and went in. Bay closed her eyes and counted to ten. She then opened her eyes and got out of the carriage. She ran as fast as she could to the side of the house, then stopped. The tool shed was built on the side of the house, she went to it, and opened the door. It was small and dark, different tools were laid about the place. It wasn't very organized but Bay managed to find a ladder, and hammer.

Bay took these tools to the side of the house. She set up the ladder, and climbed up to the place were Brien said the window was. She took the back of the hammer, and began prying out the nails, and placing the boards under her on the ladder step.

When she was done there was a small window underneath the boards. Just big enough for her to crawl through. In fact she was the only one who could crawl through, that was Brien's first part of the plan. Bay crawled through the window and fell to the attic floor. The window filled the room with grayish light. Bay pulled out the cane, and walked to the attic door. She wasn't as strong as James, but she managed to undo the latch and carefully let it down. She climbed down into the hallway, which was empty. This was the second part of the plan, to look for Lex while Brien and James stalled Rivan. She heard voices downstairs, Brien, and James were stalling. Bay could barely make out what they were saying as she went down the hall looking in the different rooms for her father.

"Come now Brien," This was Rivan's voice, "do you really expect me to believe that you only have one copy of your manuscript left?"

"I don't care what you believe Rivan," Brien said, "what I say is the truth, this is the manuscript, the very last one, I want Lex now."

"And why should I believe you?" Rivan asked.

"Because I'm through with it," Brien said, "It's not worth it over a book. I've all ready destroyed the other copies, you can have the last one." Bay paused at the third door, he sounded very convincing. She opened the door and looked inside, it was Cornelia's room, it was empty.

"I want Lex now," Brien said again. Bay opened the forth door, this was her room. Lex was sitting in a chair in the corner, his hands were tied behind his back, and his head

was bowed. "Dad!" Lex looked up and beamed.

"Bay! How did you get in here?"

"There's a window in the attic," Bay said. She went to him and began to untie him.

"Hey!" Bay jumped and looked at the door. A tall man stood in the doorway glaring at her, Bay gripped her cane tightly and raised it into the air. The man walked into the room, staring at her coldly. Bay's hands trembled, the man approached her and Bay swung at him, he dodged it and went for her again.

"Gut him Bay!" Lex ordered. Bay was too panicked to think straight, which was why she was able to do as her father asked. She brought the cane into the man's stomach. The man groaned and fell to the ground.

"Hit his head!" Lex said. Bay felt like throwing up. She turned away from the man and quickly untied Lex. He jumped up and grabbed the cane from Bay's hand and knocked the man over the head with it. He fell onto his back and was still.

"I'm sorry," Bay whispered.

"Don't be sorry Bay," Lex said. He walked over to her, and put his arms around her. Bay hugged him back tightly, "Just remember Bay," Lex said, "you have to defend yourself, they will not show pity on you, don't show pity to them. Do you understand?" Bay nodded. "It will be okay, come on."

Lex took Bay's hand and the left the room, but the people downstairs had all ready heard their fight. Rivan stood outside the door, he held a gun in his hand and a cold look in his eye. Lex stood in front of Bay and held up his cane. Bay shivered when she saw Rivan, he was a frightening man, but looking him in the eye was the most frightening thing, for they were so cold.

Bay looked at the hall behind Rivan, where were Brien and James?

Rivan pointed the gun at Lex, "Brien was lying," Rivan said, "Someone is going to tell me where the manuscript is, if you won't tell me, perhaps your daughter will." Lex could no longer contain himself. Rivan had been threatening him and his daughter, ever since he was taken hostage. Lex raised his cane ready to bring it down on Rivan's head, but Rivan over powered him by weapon standards.

The gun shot rang through the air, and Bay screamed as Lex fell onto his back, and the cane slipped from his hand to the ground. Rivan looked at Bay, and started walking toward her. Bay could only stare at his cold eyes, she couldn't look down at her father. Some where far away someone screamed, "run!" Bay turned and ran like a shot down the hallway, with Rivan right behind her.

The ladder to the attic was still open, Bay went for it, knowing it was her only way out. She grabbed the wooden ladder, and started to climb up, but Rivan was just as fast as she. He grabbed her ankle and tried to pull her down. Bay screamed again. She brought her foot up and shoved it down into Rivan's face. Rivan cried out, and loosened his grip. Bay pulled free and crawled into the attic, Rivan came after her.

Bay ran across the room to the window, her ladder was still there by the wall. She crawled through the small window and made her way down the ladder. Rivan appeared at the window and glared at her, but Bay had forgotten the tools at the top of the ladder. Rivan grabbed the hammer and began hitting it against the window frame. The wood cracked, and broke, making the hole wider. Bay crawled down the ladder as fast as she could, but Rivan reached his hand through, and grabbed it. With a hard push, the ladder began to fall away from the wall. Bay screamed and jumped off. She landed hard on the ground, the ladder fell a few feet away.

Up in the window Rivan had broken away enough wood for him to fit through. He crawled through the hole, and jumped. Bay watched in amazement, as Rivan fell through the air, and landed safely on his feet.

"Help!" Bay screamed. She jumped up and ran as fast as she could, trying to ignore the pain in her arm. Rivan ran after her. The adrenaline pumped through Bay's blood stream, her energy shot up, and Bay's legs moved faster than they ever had before. Rivan was right behind her the whole way, but Bay managed to make it to the stables.

Bay ran inside the building. She threw the door closed, and threw the latch down, locking it. She heard the loud, thump! as Rivan hit himself against the door, in an effort to get it open.

Bay could only lay on the ground trying to satisfy her need for air. Gasping, and panting, she lay on the floor resting. Her legs were sore, and her arm still hurt from the fall. Slowly her breathing became normal, and her heart slowed down, Bay was able to sit up.

Rivan's voice entered her ears from behind the door. "Do you know how you get termites out of wood work?" he asked. Bay stood up, and looked around, she knew what Rivan would do before he gave the answer.

"You smoke them out." Bay's heart began pounding again, she couldn't stay in the stables, it would burn up like gasoline-covered paper. There was only one way out.

Bay went to Ivory's pen. She let the horse out and began to saddle her. Soon the smell of smoke filled her nose, Bay coughed, but kept working. Once Ivory was saddled, she opened the pens to the other horses.

Bay could smell the fire, she looked over in the left hand corner of the stables, and saw flames appearing in the wood, eating away at it. Bay mounted Ivory and walked her to the door, she placed her hand on the latch and sighed.

"Ready for one more ride girl?" Bay asked. Ivory shifted nervously, she could smell the fire, the other horses also gathered at the door, wanting out. "Then let's go." Bay pulled the latch off, and kicked the door open.

Rivan stood there, ready for her, but he had forgotten the horses. His eyes filled with surprise when Bay appeared at the door mounted on a horse. She kicked Ivory forward, and the white horse rode forward past Rivan into the field. Bay heard gun shots behind her, but none hit her or Ivory. She didn't know why, but Bay had a feeling that Rivan missed on purpose. She looked back at him. Rivan stood in front of the burning stables, holding the gun in his hand. He did not move.

Rivan smiled to himself, "You prove to be a worthy adversary," he said to himself, "we will meet again Bay Paxon." With that Rivan turned and disappeared.

Bay rode as fast as she could back to the house. She stopped at the front door, and ran inside, dismounting Ivory. The kitchen was empty, there was a broken plate on the floor and a chair had been knocked over, but it was deserted. Bay entered the sitting room, furniture was turned over, and a glass vase was shattered. James and Brien must have put up a fight. In the corner was Roan, he was tied to a rocking chair, and gagged.

He glared at her, but Bay only glared back. She walked past him to the stairs.she felt almost too afraid to go up. But somehow her feet moved up the stairs one at a time into the hallway. Bay turned the corner and held her breath.

James and Brien sat on the floor by Lex, he was lying on his back, with one arm resting on his chest. But the first thing Bay noticed was his stomach, which rose up and down slowly, he was breathing.

"Dad!" Bay rushed forward. James and Brien looked up in surprise.

"He is all right Bay," Brien said. Bay sat down on the floor next to Lex. He smiled at her. A piece of cloth was tied around his shoulder, above the bullet wound.

"I'm all right Bay, it's just my shoulder. Are you okay?" Bay nodded.

"I ran from Rivan. But, the stables are on fire, Rivan burned them," James flinched a little, "the horses are all right," Bay assured him. "Come on dad, you need a doctor."

"It's all right Bay," Brien said, "I have basic medical training, I know how to care for a bullet wound." Brien gently took Lex by the arms, and James took his legs. They carried him to Bay's room, and laid him on the bed.

"What about Roan?" Bay asked, "what is he doing here?"

"He is going to give us information on Rivan," Brien said.

"He will?" Bay asked confused.

"Well, maybe not willingly, but he will never the less. James, go downstairs and watch him. Bay you can help me with Lex, we need to get that bullet out of his shoulder." Lex groaned a little, but Bay nodded. James left the room, and Brien began taking off Lex's clothes. Brien cut the sleeve off Lex's coat, and shirt so that he could remove them without hurting his arm. He then removed his shoes, and belt around his pants.

"All right Bay, I need you to get me a small, and very sharp knife from the kitchen, and something we can get the bullet out

61

with, pliers, or tweezers, something like that. Get a bucket of hot water, fresh towels, two pairs of rubber gloves, a needle and thread, and we need something to put him to sleep. Is there any ether in this house?"

"I don't know," Bay said, "I'll ask James."

"Okay, get all that stuff, quickly. I need to stay here and make sure he doesn't bleed to death." Bay nodded she kissed her father's sweaty forehead and left the room. She first went to the kitchen and started boiling some water in a kettle. She then went to the bathroom an found fresh towels. Once again in the kitchen Bay pulled out a series of knifes Brien could use. She also found two pairs of rubber gloves. Cornelia, and Delon used these when ever they washed dishes. While the water boiled, Bay went upstairs to Cornelia's room, where she found a box of sewing supplies. Now there were only two more things.

Bay solved the pliers easily. They did not have any in the house, but in the bathroom, Bay found a pair of Cornelia's eyebrow tweezers, perfect for removing a bullet. But now they needed the most important item that would be the hardest to obtain. James was in the living room, resting on the couch.

"James?" Bay approached him, and he opened his eyes. "We need something to put my father to sleep so we can get the bullet out, do we have anything here?" James thought about it carefully, then nodded.

"I have a bottle of chloroform. We used it when ever I had to perform a surgery on one of the horses. Luckily it's not in the stables, I'll go get it." James got up and left the room. Bay stood in the sitting room alone, except for Roan. Bay looked at him again, he stared at her coldly, but Bay was no longer afraid of him, she turned her head and ignored him.

James appeared once again holding a bottle of chloroform in his hand. He handed it to Bay. "Don't worry, Brien is a good doctor. Your father will be all right." Bay smiled.

"Thanks James." She carried all the equipment upstairs into the bedroom. Brien was holding a cloth over Lex's wound, though the bleeding had almost stopped.

"Good work," Brien said, "now let's get started, I hope you are not afraid of blood." Bay shook her head. Brien poured some of the water from the kettle into a bowl and washed his hands. He dumped this water out the window, refilled it, and had Bay wash her hands. Brien pulled on the pair of gloves, and Bay put on the second pair.

"All right buddy," Brien said, he picked up a towel and soaked it in the chloroform, "count backwards from one hundred Lex." Brien put the towel to Lex's mouth, Lex closed his eyes and mumbled out the numbers, "One hundred, ninety-nine, ninety-eight, ninety-seven...." Lex's voice became smaller and began to drift off, "ninety-six....ninety-five....." Then he was in a deep sleep. Brien removed the cloth and put it aside. He studied the knifes Bay had brought, and selected a small thin one. Brien sighed and placed the metal to Lex's wound. Bay wanted to look away, but she forced herself to watch.

Brien cut a X shape on the bullet wound, and gently moved the skin aside. He held out his hand, and Bay handed him the tweezers. Brien clutched the tool tightly, and began to slid the tweezers into the hole, Bay used a cloth to keep the blood from flowing out to quickly. Brien put the tweezers in deep, his own fingers went into the wound. Bay's hands started to tremble, she bit down on her tongue to stay focused, and continued to monitor the blood.

"Got it," Brien whispered. Bay looked up and watched Brien pull his fingers, then the tweezers out of the wound. Clutched between the tongs was a small, metal, bullet. Bay sighed with relief and happiness. Brien put the tweezers, and bullet on the bedside table.

Brien took off his gloves and Bay placed a new cloth over the wound. Brien turned and opened Cornelia's sewing box. He selected a needle and thread, and wove it quickly. Bay moved the cloth and Brien began sewing up the wound. Bay winced as she saw the needle poke through the skin, an pull the thread through, but she bit her tongue again, and continued to watch.

Brien finished sewing the wound. He then dabbed it with alcohol, and cut a piece of cloth to place over the wound, Brien found some material, and wrapped Lex's arm. It was finally done.

Bay sighed deeply and collapsed into a chair. Brien wiped the sweat from his brow and smiled at her. "You did good kid." Bay smiled back. "Come on let's clean up."

Bay stood up and took off her gloves. She helped Brien change the bed sheets, wash the tools, and put everything away.

"You might want to sew up Lex's clothes, I know he likes that jacket," Brien said. Bay nodded and gathered up her father's clothes. Brien covered the sleeping man with a blanket, and they quietly left the room.

Bay followed Brien to the sitting room, where James was dosing on the couch, and Roan was struggling to get out of his bindings.

"No need to do that," Brien said coldly, "you and I are going to have a little talk." Brien approached Roan and removed his gag.

"What makes you think I will tell you anything?" Roan spat at him. Brien gave him a sly smile, "I have my ways." Brien untied him, and took his arm.

"Stay here Bay," Brien said, "see if you can wake up James and make some lunch, okay?" Bay nodded, mystified. Brien dragged Roan away from the sitting room into the study. With a snap of the door, and the click of a lock they were gone, and Bay could only wonder what could possibly be happening on the other side.

Chapter Six

Two men sat opposite of each other, staring into their eyes. Both were men of strong will and physical strength, and both had intelligence. The main difference was that one was good, and one was evil. And though they were both equally intelligent, one learned more than the other ever could.

Brien sat patiently looking at Roan. Roan looked angry, and distrustful. When Rivan had heard Lex and the second man struggling upstairs he had ordered Roan, and a second man with him to kill James, and capture Brien. But the tables turned ironically when James had manage to kill his man, and Brien captured Roan. In the struggle Rivan went upstairs, and shot Lex.

Outside it started to rain, any fire left from the stable would be put out. Brien and Roan continued to watch each other silently, but Brien waited until Roan's face began to relax, and his muscles untense.

"You are a traitor Roan," Brien said, "you lied to Delon, so that you could live in this house and spy on them, you broke her heart." Roan said nothing.

"Dante said that betrayers are sent to the deepest circle of Hell, there your soul shall be eaten over and over by the weeping Lucifer for eternity."

"That is a book, Ink," Roan finally spoke, "you spend more time in them than you do your real life." Brien merely smiled.

"Book or no book a similar punishment awaits you in Hell, unless you help free your soul." Roan smirked.

"And how might a free my soul? By telling you what you want, then I shall die and go to the kingdom of Heaven?" Roan chuckled. Brien shook his head.

"There are many ways of freeing your soul, baptism, confession, I am sure that you can do all of these, turn to a church, move to a new town, perhaps even start a family, it would be your choice."

"And so you let me go and I begin this new life of redemption," Roan said, "in exchange for what?"

"Nothing," Brien said, "but Roan I do not know what you would do if I let you go, you would either rejoin Rivan, or start a new life. I need some way for you to prove it. You can help prove it by giving me the answer to this question, which story is Rivan's?"

Roan looked at him in genuine confusion, "what do you mean?"

"In the manuscript, why does Rivan want to destroy my book, which story is his?" Roan stared at him.

"You don't know?" Brien shook his head.

"If you do not answer me truthfully, or do not answer me at all, I shall turn you into the police, and tell them all that has happened. But if you do tell me truthfully I will let you go." Roan looked at him in surprise, he then looked at his hands. Brien placed his hand on Roan's wrist, he could feel his pulse beating normally.

"Rivan is a traitor as well," Brien said, "he left you here." Roan remained silent, Brien studied Roan's hand.

"You were married once," Brien said, Roan stared at him in surprise, "I can see the mark on your finger were the wedding band was. I don't know what happened to your wife Roan, but

66

having a life like this is no way to run from the memory."

Roan continued to look at his hand, Brien kept his fingers on his wrist. Nearly a whole minute past before Roan finally spoke.

"Rivan was responsible for a series of murders in Germany, he murdered over twelve people in a small village there, his father had been tried for murder and executed there. Rivan wanted revenge for his father, so he killed the jurors that convicted him, and some of their family members."

"The Shireville Murders," Brien whispered out the name of the story, and village Roan had referred to. Brien remembered the day he had stayed in Shireville Germany, the people told him of the sixteen murders that had taken place there. All the victim's throats had been cut, almost decapitated. The towns people believed it was the doings of a ghost.

"Why do you think that?" Brien had asked them.

"Because," an elderly man answered, "years ago, a family of seven was murdered, there throats had been cut in the same style. We caught the man who did it, Joah Hydenburg, and executed him. Now his ghost has come back for revenge against the people who convicted him, and their family members. Once they are dead his soul will rest."

It wasn't Joah Hydenburg's ghost that had killed those people, it was his son, Rivan Hydenburg. Rivan had discovered that Brien had found the story and wanted to destroy it. That was it.

Brien let go of Roan's hand, he was telling the truth. "All right Roan, a deal is a deal. Go." Brien stood up and went to the door. He unlocked it and stepped out, Roan followed.

Bay and James were in the kitchen eating some vegetable soup Bay had made. Bay watched in horror as Brien opened the front door, and Roan left.

"What are you doing?" Bay cried. Brien took her hands.

"It's okay Bay, he is not going back to Rivan."

"How do you know?" Bay demanded.

"Roan told me all I need to know, he wasn't lying, I listened to his pulse while he told me the story, it remained normal. I know Roan will not return to Rivan, because Rivan betrayed him. You need to trust me Bay, do you?" Bay hesitated, she looked out the window and watched as Roan walked down the road towards town, his head was bowed. Bay nodded her head.

"Good," Brien smiled at her. "Do I smell soup?" Bay made a bowl for Brien, then poured a second one. She put a slice of bread in it, made a glass of water, and carried them upstairs to Lex's room.

Lex was almost awake when she came in. His eyes were fluttering, and he made a small groaning noise.

"Dad?" Bay set the soup down and sat on a chair next to the bed. Lex breathed deeply and opened his eyes.

"Bay," he whispered smiling, "how's my girl?" Bay smiled.

"Are you feeling better?" She asked.

"Just a little," Lex said, "what's happened since I was out?"

"Rivan chased me to the stables, and burned it down, but I got all the horses out all right. Brien captured Roan, he interrogated Roan in the study, and he got him to tell us about Rivan, I don't know how." Lex chuckled.

"Brien is full of secrets," he said.

"So are you," Bay said, "why didn't you tell me you were Brien's friend?" Bay asked.

"I had to protect you Bay, Brien was always on the run from his enemies, I couldn't let them find you. So I help Brien in secret, I couldn't tell you about him."

"You shouldn't have lied to me," Bay said. Lex raised his arm and touched her cheek.

"You are everything to me Bay, the last thing I want is to hurt you, or lie to you. But I would rather do that than put you in danger of any kind. When you grow up and have a child you will understand me, there is no love that equals that between a parent and child. I love you Bay." Bay hugged him and kissed his cheek, she could never stay mad at her father over anything.

"You did a good job on my arm," Lex said. Bay helped him

sit up, and handed him the soup. Lex ate it as if he hadn't eaten in days. When he was done he laid back down on the bed. Bay stayed with him until he was asleep once again.

Bay took the empty bowl and went downstairs. Brien was sitting at the table in deep thought, James was gone.

"Where is James?" Bay asked putting the dishes in the sink.

"He went outside to check on the horses and the stable," Brien answered. Bay washed her hands and sat down beside him.

"I guess it's over," she mumbled.

"What do you mean?" Brien asked.

"Rivan has run away, and your last copy of the lost manuscript is destroyed."

"Oh no Bay, nothing is over, it has just begun."

"What do you mean?" Bay asked.

"I couldn't tell anyone, not even Lex. The notebook I gave you, Rivan did destroy it, but it was not the last manuscript.

"There is one last copy of the Lost Manuscript still out there."

PART TWO

Chapter Seven

The sun rose in the sky spreading light, and warmth over the Hinten Farm. Bay sat in the window sill watching the different morning colors play across the sky. She watched for almost a hour, until the sun was completely visible. She turned her head and looked at Lex sleeping peacefully on the bed. She smiled, her heart was light, she had her father back, safe.

Lex didn't wake up so Bay stood and left the room quietly. Brien was, of course, all ready awake. Bacon was frying in a skillet, and coffee was brewing. Bay inhaled the sweet smelling air and sat down at the table. Brien smiled at her but did not speak. Bay wondered if something was troubling him. Brien placed some bacon on a plate along with a slice of toast and placed it before her. Bay poured herself a glass of orange juice and nibbled at her food.

The two of them were very silent, Bay didn't know what to say, and Brien knew exactly what to say, as most silent people do, but he kept it to himself. Brien was usually a quiet person, though he always had something to say, sometimes. There are just times when you no longer care for human voices, and simply enjoy the silence that so rarely comes.

Bay was also a quiet person, but sometimes silences scared her, she wanted Brien's warm voice to enter her ear and tell her everything would be all right. Rivan will not bother us anymore. I will get my book published, and you and your father can finally live together in peace. But none of these words came to her, because they were not true. Rivan would be back, and there was still a long road to getting Brien's book published. It seemed that all good things had a long and hard road to travel.

Brien sat down with a cup of coffee, he had a leather note book in his hand. He pulled out a pen and began writing in the pages. The scratching sound of the pen on paper was the only sound. Bay stared at Brien, she suddenly realized that he was the only writer she had ever met. She loved reading books, but she never considered that someone had sat down and wrote them all down, pulling the words from their minds, and imagination. How does Brien do that? Bay thought to herself, I wish I could do that.

Bay sucked air in then slowly let it out. Brien didn't look up. Bay finally spoke, "Where is the last manuscript?" she asked.

"I can't tell you," Brien said not looking up from his booklet.

"Why not?" Bay asked. She felt disappointment. She wanted Brien to look at her with his dark green eyes, to notice her, not just hear her.

"I need to protect you from Rivan. If he knows that you know were the book is he will try to make you tell him were it is."

"I wouldn't tell him!" Bay said. She felt sadness as well, Brien didn't trust her. Brien looked up at her kindly. Bay felt her heart skip when he looked at her.

"I know you wouldn't Bay, willingly. But you have never been tortured. Your hands have not been tied with leather straps, squeezing into your flesh. Red-hot metal has never touched your delicate skin, nor has the sting of a whip, and a razor has never sliced open your flesh." Bay felt her stomach turn over, her eyes never left Brien's. "have... you been tortured before?" Bay asked carefully. Brien stood up and pulled off his shirt. Bay felt tears fill up her eyes when she saw large brown marks on his skin from burns, and long red streaks from a whip's evil touch all over Brien's back. Brien turned and Bay saw a long scar travel from his shoulder and stop at his stomach. Bay's hands trembled, a tear slid down her cheek, she quickly wiped it away.

"Razor scar," Brien mumbled. He pulled his shirt back on. "I can't let that happen to you Bay. I'm sorry you had to see that, but you need to know." Brien walked over to her, he put his arm around her shoulders. Bay laid her head on his chest. Brien rubbed her back. He kissed her forehead.

"It will be okay though," he said. He touched her head and sat down again.

"Can you tell me what happened?" Bay asked in a careful whisper, "you know, when you were tortured? If you can't I understand." Brien leaned back in his chair thoughtfully. Brien told Bay his first story, one that was in the Lost Manuscript actually. Bay listened carefully as the words came out of his mouth in perfect detail.

"I had just left Sweden. I didn't really know were I was going next, the manuscript was almost finished. I knew there were only a few more stories I needed to collect before it was done. I was staying at an Inn in Germany, it was just a small out-of-the-way place, and I was sleeping very well, but at midnight I was awoken when a hand suddenly placed itself over my mouth. I opened my eyes and saw Rivan for the first time. I first thought it was one of the murderers I had caught, and that they were here for revenge.

" 'you should have stayed out of other person's business writer,' he said. He placed a cloth over my mouth and I was rendered unconscious. When I woke up I was in a very dark room. I was shirtless, and freezing cold. My hands were tied above my head to a long pole, and a belt held my waist to it, I was also gagged.

"It was completely dark in the room, I wondered if I was having a nightmare. Then a single light came on. It was a lonely light bulb hanging from the ceiling. Rivan stood underneath it sitting in a chair, about five of his men were circled around me. Rivan stood up and removed my gag. 'You found my story,' Rivan said, 'tell me where your book is and I will let you go.' I said no. At the time I was still trying to figure out which story was Rivan's.

"First they used whips. Without warning a man let one down on my back, it was the most horrible thing I had ever experienced. Just a thin piece of leather cutting my back open, and blood running down it like a fountain. the first strike I thought that the whip had cut open my back, and the skin had been ripped off. Rivan asked me again, but I couldn't answer if I wanted to I could only breath and wonder if I would die. I thought I was going to die in that dark hole. They whipped me two more times. I thought someone might hear me because I was screaming so loud, I still don't know why no one did.

"They used fire next. Someone lit a match and simply held it to my skin. I wanted to tell him, I wanted to tell him everything, where the manuscript was, who I was. I would have told him the events of my live from beginning to end, I would have told them my school teachers name if they asked. But there was just a little light of sanity in my brain telling me not to. So I just started speaking rubbish. I gave out famous quotes in Latin, then I started reading out Shakespeare, Julius Caesar mostly. I don't think they could make out what I said because I was screaming. They stopped and Rivan stood up holding a razor, he asked me where the manuscript was again. I almost told him, I opened my mouth and said, 'it's in.... Tale-tale Heart! Pit and the Pendulum!...' I simply started screaming out Edgar Allen Poe stories. Rivan placed the razor to my skin, and I started screaming, 'THE RAVEN! THE RAVEN! THE RAVEN!....' I could only say that one because I had forgotten the others, and Rivan started cutting me. He did it slowly, to make it more painful.

"I came to myself and kicked him squarely in the testicles

before he could get past my stomach. Rivan fell to the floor, and his men came to his aid. I took my chance, my hands were covered in sweat, and I was able to pull my hands free. I learned how to from an escape artist once. I untied myself and ran like the devil was chasing me. I don't remember much, just stairs and darkness. I found a door and I ran outside. It was night time, I remember how cold it was, and I just kept running, because I knew one of them was right behind me, ready to grab me and drag me back to that dark room in the ground and torture me again. I ran on until my heart was about to burst out of my chest, I fell to the ground and went unconscious again.

"I woke up in a hospital the next morning. Someone had found me in the street, naked and bleeding. I hid out in a small village after that, for almost a month. I still have nightmares about that night." Brien drank deeply from his coffee, Bay looked down at her hands.

"You didn't have to tell me," She said.

"Sometimes you need to tell people things like that, so that you don't forget."

"Why would you want to remember?" Bay asked.

"Someone once said, 'If we do not learn from history we shall repeat it.'" Brien said. He sighed and began writing in his notebook again. Bay didn't say anything, she almost wished she had not said anything in the first place.

A few minutes later Lex appeared in the room. Bay smiled, and hugged him. "I heard a rumor there was coffee," Lex said. Brien smiled and poured him a cup.

"How are you feeling?" Brien asked. Lex sat at the table and yawned.

"I've had better, but you did a good job on the arm."

"Thank Bay, she helped a great deal." Lex smiled and played with Bay's hair.

"Hidden talent's," Lex said. He drank his coffee and ate some bacon.

"Where is James?" Bay asked.

"He went out to the stables, to see how much damage was

done." Bay finished her breakfast and went outside. She jogged across the field to the stables.

The fire had eaten away most of it. Two walls still stood, burnt wood was scattered all over the field, and the smell of smoke filled the air. James was amounst the rubble, he picked up any burnt wood and through it into a pile. Bay ran to him.

"I'm sorry James," she said. James turned and looked at her sadly.

"It's not your fault," he said. "Rivan did this." James picked up a horseshoe that had survived and put it in a small pile of items that had also survived, a rake, shovel, more horseshoes, two saddles, reins, and a brush. Bay walked through the rubble beside James. She picked up burnt wood and threw it into the pile. She found a comb used for brushing horse manes, and another pair of reins. They both worked all morning cleaning the area. Soon the wood was stacked, and the surviving items were all found. Bay helped James gather the horses and secure them to trees so that they could be brushed.

"Don't worry James, we can rebuild the stables," Bay said.

"I know," James said, "I'm just worried about where we can keep the horses until then. I guess we can tie them to a tree and throw blankets over them." Bay nodded and ran her brush through Midnight's coat.

It was almost eleven o'clock when they finished. James took Bay's arm and led her across the field.

"I didn't get any breakfast," he said, "what do you say we have an early lunch?" Bay nodded in agreement. The mood of the place seemed to lighten, until they entered the house.

Lex and Brien were arguing about something. There was no shouting, and both were sitting, but they were clearly not agreeing about something.

"What's wrong?" Bay asked when she entered.

"We are discussing a plan of action," Lex said, "or trying." Brien sighed deeply and rubbed his eyes.

"We need to go to Germany," Brien said, "To Rivan's town. 'Keep your friends close and your enemies closer.' I want to learn as much of Rivan as I can."

"We need to find the manuscript and get it to the publishing company you found," Lex said, "this might be the one."

"Rivan will be following us," Brien said, "the moment we get the manuscript they will appear and take it away. I have to be careful, it's the very last copy, if we don't get it, it could take me months to rewrite the book, maybe even years."

Lex sighed deeply and rubbed his temples. Bay only watched the two men with curiosity, wondering which one would decide her fate.

"Lex, you have to trust me. I know Rivan, we have to lose him before we go for the manuscript, we can do that if we go to Germany. Please come with me Lex, I have never brought you down the wrong path." Lex stared at Brien for a long time. Bay held her breath until her father finally nodded.

"All right Brien, I'm going to trust you, I always have, but this is different. My daughter is here this time."

"Does that mean I can come?" Bay asked hopefully. Lex closed his eyes and nodded.

"As much as I hate to, I know that the only way to protect you is to keep you with me, so yes, you are coming."

Bay knew all the dangers awaiting on this journey, but she couldn't think about it, she could only think of the adventure, away from the Hinten Farm, with her father, and with Brien. Just like the things she read in her books, the things she had always dreamed of being apart of.

"When are we leaving?" Bay asked.

"I am going to town later to see when the next train leaves," Lex said.

"I will come with you," James said, "none of us should go out on our own."

"Are you coming with us?" Bay asked.

"I'm still thinking about it," James said, "but I most likely will." Bay smiled, her heart felt light once again. She turned and began making lunch.

After they ate some leftover soup, and sandwiches Lex and James took the horses and rode into town. Brien and Bay took the carriage, they decided it was time Cornelia, and Delon came back home. Bay sat in the front with Brien watching the country side roll by. The afternoon was warm, and the air was fresh. They were both silent, Bay wanted to find something to talk about though. She pondered for a moment then said, "What is Germany like?" Brien shrugged.

"It's like any other place, nice country. Shireville is very small, I was spending the night there, I didn't really expect to find a story, but stories are everywhere. Hiding out in small places, waiting for someone to find them."

"Will you write our story?" Bay asked, "about Rivan, and this adventure?" Brien nodded.

"Most likely, I'm sure this will make a good story." Bay nodded. They were silent for a moment then Brien said.

"Maybe you should write it." Bay looked up in surprise.

"Write what? This adventure?" Brien nodded.

"I couldn't, I don't know how to write a story." Brien chuckled.

"You can't be taught to write a story Bay, you are either born with it or not. The only way to find out is to give it a try."

"Could you always write stories?" Bay asked.

"I use to tell my father stories, and my mom when I was little. My dad taught me how to read and write, I wrote my first chapter book when I was thirteen, and I wrote a lot of short stories." Bay mused for a moment still wondering if Brien was right, if she should try and write something.

"Brien, is Rivan the only person after you?" Bay asked.

"No, a murderer from Spain has been trying to track me down as well. When I learned his story I helped the police capture him, and so he has been after me for revenge."

"That's awful!" Bay gasped. Brien only chuckled.

"He won't find me, he is not as smart, or as connected as Rivan is."

"Rivan is awful keen on getting your book," Bay said.

"You would be too if it revealed how you and your father murdered almost twenty people in one town." Bay nodded in agreement.

Her house appeared in the distance. Bay watched it and smiled, there truly was no place like home. Brien stopped the carriage and jumped off, Bay followed, but something didn't seem right, the house was quiet, there was no smoke coming from the chimney, and no lights in the windows. Brien seemed to sense something wrong as well. He went to the door and looked into the window, all was dark and quiet inside.

Brien opened the door and Bay followed. Her mouth dropped when she saw what had happened. The table in the kitchen was turned over, and some of the windows were broken. Glass littered the floor, chairs were shattered into pieces, and large scratches were carved into the walls. Bay could only stare at the destruction. Brien laid a comforting hand on her shoulder.

"Stay here," he whispered. Brien left the kitchen, with Bay standing there staring at the mess. Without really thinking about it Bay pushed the table back and started stacking the broken wood, and gathering the glass. Rivan had done this, as a warning to Lex, but what had he done to Cornelia and Delon?

Bay's hands began to tremble, she dropped a large piece of glass and a cut appeared on her palm. A drop of blood ran down her hand. Bay sighed and grabbed a cleaning cloth to tie around her cut. Bay sat on the ground and a tear ran down her cheek, this was her home, and Rivan had tore it up.

Bay looked at the piece of glass with a little blood on it, and she suddenly felt anger. Rivan was evil, look what he had done to Brien, and Lex, and her. Bay picked up the glass and studied it thoughtfully. Her own thoughts scared her, what she would like to do with the glass. Bay shook her head and threw the glass away. But she couldn't throw away her thoughts.

Brien had searched the second floor of the house. It too was wrecked, furniture was turned over, things were scratched in the walls, in the middle of the hall was a picture of Bay sitting in a tree, someone had stuck it to the wall with a knife, the blade stuck out of her head. Brien glared at the knife and pulled it out of the wall. The picture fluttered lazily to the ground. Brien picked it up, there was a cut in the middle of

Bay's smiling face where the knife had been. Brien put the photo in his pocket and attached the knife to his belt, he would use it later, and not for pictures.

Brien searched for awhile then went back downstairs to the cellar. It was very dark down in the basement, and there was no light. Brien found a lantern and matches on the stairs of the cellar. He lit it and made his way down into the dark room.

The stairs creaked under his weight, and the cool underground air touched his skin. Brien held the lantern forward and called out quietly. "Cornelia? Delon?" Brien whispered, his voice echoed in the room, his only answer was his voice bouncing off the walls.

Suddenly the door slammed shut. Brien spun around, a man stood on top of the stairs in front of the door. Blocking the way out. Brien turned again. A second lantern had been lit, Rivan stood holding it up with a pleased smile on his face. Two other men stood behind him. Brien always had a habit of nicknaming Rivan's goons, it gave him a small pleasure when he ever had to meet them. For these three he mentally called them Cue, as in cue-ball, for the man at the stairs was bald, the second man was called Slim, he was a very tall and thin man. The third man was simply called Red, he was a very big man, with muscles bulging out of his body, and his face was as red as a tomato.

"I had a good feeling you would come back here," Rivan said, "I figured I could give you a welcoming."

"Aren't you a peach," Brien said, Rivan only smiled. "Where are the girls?" Brien demanded.

"They are a little tied up at the moment," Rivan said, his smile widened, and Brien glared at him. His hand went to the knife at his belt. With a flash he pulled it out and threw it at Rivan. But Rivan saw it coming, he ducked to the floor and the knife plunged into the wall behind him.

"I'm impressed Brien," Rivan said standing up again, "your aim and speed have improved since the last we met."

"What do you want?" Brien cut him off. Rivan gave him a sarcastically confused look.

"Doesn't this little room bring back memories?" Rivan asked. Brien felt his heart sink into his stomach, he wanted to vomit his heart back up. Rivan saw the fear in his eyes and he gave a smile of pure evil. Memories indeed.

Red and Slim lunged forward and grabbed Brien's arms. His lantern fell and rolled away. Brien struggled furiously in an effort to escape. Red raised his fist and brought it into Brien's stomach. Brien groaned in pain, his legs went limp and he thought that he really would vomit. Red and Slim dragged him across the room and threw him into a chair. Slim began to bound his wrists. Brien started to pull away, but Red raised a fist again and punched Brien hard in the face. Brien's neck jerked back, and blood dripped from his nose.

Rivan pulled up a chair and sat in front of him. Red held up the lantern in Brien's face. Brien blinked and squinted, beads of sweat formed on his brow.

"You know what's coming Ink," Rivan said coldly, "Save yourself the pain and tell me where the manuscript is." Brien realized that they didn't know about Bay, if they had she would be down here with him. Brien didn't answer Rivan, he began working with his bindings, but Slim pulled out a knife and held it to his neck.

"If you mess with those again I'll cut your throat," Brien let his hands go limp.

"Where is it Ink?" Rivan demanded. Brien couldn't stop himself, he formed spittle in his mouth and spat it into Rivan's face. Rivan winced and quickly wiped it out of his eyes. Red stepped forward and punched Brien's face once again, then his stomach. Brien cried out and coughed loudly. He silently prayed to God to make Bay leave the house. Please God, Brien begged, I don't care if you leave me here, or if I die in this hole, just make sure Bay leaves, please, please...

"What would you like first Brien?" Rivan asked cutting off Brien's thoughts. Rivan was now standing, glaring at him.

"I personally like the razor, we could finish up that scar on your chest. Or I could carve my name in your flesh, maybe then you won't forget my abilities." Rivan tore Brien's shirt away and placed the cold metal to his skin. Brien's heart pounded and sweat ran down his face. Rivan stared at him with his cold eyes.

"Last chance," he said. Brien felt the urge to scream out the location of the manuscript, but instead he bit down on his tongue. Rivan pressed the razor to his flesh and began to cut it open slowly, blood ran down his skin, and Brien began to scream.

In the kitchen Bay looked up from the floor, she heard Brien's scream echo through the whole house. She jumped up, her mind full of fear. Bay ran out of the kitchen, but stopped herself. The scream had come from the cellar, but she couldn't go down unarmed.

Bay ran back to the kitchen she picked up a chair leg and gave it a practice swing. She spotted a large piece of glass on the floor that she had missed. Bay picked it up as well and put it in her pocket. She ran to the cellar door and held up the chair leg like a baseball bat. Bay breathed in deeply, she clutched the wood tightly.

"Come on Bay," she whispered to herself, "you have to do this." Bay gritted her teeth. Mustering all her strength and courage Bay kicked the door, with a snap it flew open. Cue spun around and glared at her. Bay swung the chair leg hitting his arm. Cue cried out in pain and clutched his arm. Bay took her chance and hit his head. Cue went off balance and fell down the stairs to the cold ground. Bay ran down them and jumped over him.

Brien was tied to a chair at the other end of the room, his shirt was torn away and blood was running down his stomach, and face. Rivan stood standing over him holding a bloody razor in his hand.

Bay no longer felt fear, there was too much anger, too much hate. All she wanted to do was kill Rivan.

"You BASTARD!" Bay screamed. She ran forward and swung the chair leg as hard as she could at his face. The wood connected with bone and Rivan fell to the ground. Red stepped forward. Bay swung at him, but Red grabbed the chair leg and yanked it out of her hands. Bay felt her body tremble as Red grabbed her neck, and squeeze, cutting off her air supply.

Choking and gasping, Bay reached into her pocket and pulled out the shard of glass. Bay brought it down on Red's hand. He screamed and let go of her neck. Bay gasped and breathed again. Slim ran forward and grabbed Bay. He spun her around and wrapped his arms around her shoulders and neck. Bay raised the glass and brought it down into Slims leg.

Slim gasped and fell to the ground clutching his leg and staring wide eyed at the piece of glass sticking out of it. Bay ran past him to Brien. Brien was panting hard, and blood stained his chest. Bay quickly untied his straps. Brien lifted his shaking hands. He took his shirt and tied it around the cut in his chest. It ran from his left rib, to the right. It was deep, and wide. Bay felt sick when she saw all the blood. Brien stood up and grabbed her arm. But Red grabbed Bay's other arm.

"Not so fast." he growled. Brien pulled Bay away from him and punched his face, Red stumbled backward. He tripped over Slim, who was nursing his leg. Red fell on top of the lantern that he had been holding, suddenly his entire backside was covered in kerosene, and set afire.

Red let out a horrible scream and began rolling around on the floor trying to put the fire out. He rolled over and bumped into a pile of fire wood that Lex kept down in the basement for when winter came. The wood caught fire and began to burn.

Brien grabbed Bay's hand and pulled her forward. They ran out of the cellar, back outside where the carriage still awaited them. Brien stumbled and almost fell. Bay put his arm over her shoulders and helped him into the carriage.

"Wait," Brien whimpered, "Cornelia, Delon...They are still in the house." Bay gasped and ran back into the kitchen. She looked around the room desperately, the house was already filled with the smell of fire, and smoke was coming out of the cellar. In desperation, Bay opened the study door. Cornelia and Delon were both sitting on the floor with their hands and feet tied, and their mouths gagged. Bay ran forward and untied Cornelia.

"Bay!" She gasped, "it's a trap, Rivan is in the cellar..."

"I know, it's too late," Bay said. She began untying Delon, "the house is on fire, the carriage is outside, we have to hurry." The two women jumped up and followed Bay out of the room. Rivan stood in the cellar door rubbing his head. Cue was behind him. He saw them leave the room and pointed a long accusing finger at Bay. Bay screamed in surprise and the three girls ran as fast as they could into the kitchen, and out the door. Cue ran after them.

"I'll get you for that!" He screamed at Bay. Bay gasped and ran to the carriage. Cornelia and Delon jumped into the passenger seat, and Bay climbed into the driver's.

Cue ran out of the house and ran to them. Bay whipped the reins as hard as she could, "Get! Get!" she cried at the horses. The horses took off as fast as they could. Cue tried to jump onto the carriage, but he was too slow. The carriage took off at full speed down the road. Bay turned her head and watched Rivan and Cue stare after them. Behind the men the house was turning into fire, smoke floated into the air, and flames ate at the wood. Bay looked away, her home was gone, Lex was all she had left now. Bay stared at the long road, and cried silently.

Chapter Eight

Bay drove the carriage as fast as the horses could take it, back to the Hinten Farm. Cornelia and Delon helped her carry Brien inside. Brien had lost a lot of blood, and was beginning to pass out. Luckily Lex and James were back from town. They took Brien and carried him upstairs to a bedroom. This time it was Lex's turn to operate.

Bay fetched some warm water and towels, and brought Cornelia's sewing kit upstairs. James stayed downstairs taking care of Delon and Cornelia. "Help Lex," James said, "I'll make some tea, go on." Bay went upstairs with the necessaries. Lex cleaned the blood away from Brien's skin. Bay monitored the blood coming out of the wound while Lex sewed it up. Once the wound was closed, Lex dabbed alcohol on it and wrapped linen around Brien's body, from his chest to the stomach. Brien slept on the bed when they were done.

"Will he be all right?" Bay asked quietly.

"There was some blood loss, but I think he will be fine," Lex said, "what happened Bay? Are you all right?"

Bay told him fully what happened at the house, at the end her voice started to tremble.

"The house is gone," Bay said pathetically, "it caught fire when the lantern broke," Bay felt tears coming to her eyes again, but she held them back.

"It's okay Bay," Lex said, "We can move to a new house, I have some money saved. Everything will be all right, I promise." Lex sat on the daybed next to her and hugged her tightly. Bay laid her head on his chest, and wrapped her arms around his waist. Lex rocked her gently and hummed a familiar lullaby. Bay sighed with relief, happy to be back, safe, in her father's arms. When the lullaby was over Lex said, "We planned on leaving tomorrow on the morning train, but we could go tonight, what do you think?"

"The farther we are from Rivan, the better," Bay said.

"All right, when Brien wakes up we can leave. Go on and pack your things." Lex kissed her cheek. Bay stood and started to leave the room.

"Bay," Lex called as she opened the door. Bay stopped and looked at him. "There was no wrong in what you did Bay, down in the cellar, you had to protect yourself and Brien. Do you understand?" Bay nodded and forced a smile.

"I love you dad."

"I love you too angel." Bay left and went back outside to the carriage. She had left her bag in it the previous day. She took the bag and went to her room. She was thankful for the quiet of the house, though she kept glancing nervously out onto the road, afraid she would see Rivan and his men riding toward them.

The road remained deserted, and Bay packed extra clothing, she also found room for a few more books. Bay left her room and decided to go to the attic again. She was tired of the five books she read over and over. Bay opened the attic door and climbed up into the room. She no longer needed the candle, the new window filled the attic with light. Bay stood up and went towards the pile of books. She was about to sit down and go through them once again, when a soft voice entered her ear.

"Bay? What are you doing here?" Bay turned around and saw Delon standing in the corner holding a large black box.

"I was going to pack some books for the journey, can I?"

"Of course!" Delon said. "Most of these are Brien's, they are excellent reading, you take whatever you wish." Bay smiled, and hugged her. Delon put down the box she was holding and hugged her back.

"I'm going to miss you Bay. Promise you will be careful, and visit us when you get back."

"I will," Bay said. "What do you have in that box?" Delon sat down on the floor and placed the box in front of her. Bay sat down as well.

"I was going to give it back to Brien," Delon said. She opened the lid, inside was a small typewriter. The keys stuck out longingly, each printed with a letter or symbol. Bay ran her fingers over the keys she longed to press them and hear the clicking of the ink hitting the paper.

"Is this Brien's?" Bay asked.

"Yes, he use to type on it all day. He would sneak up to the attic when no one noticed and I would sit in my room just listening to the typing. I even used the pattern of the key strokes to write a song once." Bay laughed and smiled at the typewriter.

"Do you think Brien would teach me how to type?" she asked.

"Certainly! Brien loves to teach. I remember him giving James reading lessons up in the stable loft." Delon smiled to herself, reliving a distant memory. "Cornelia never cared much for children, but I always love having Brien, James, and you around." Delon replaced the lid covering the typewriter. She picked up the box and stood up.

"I will go deliver this, you help yourself to the books." With that Delon walked out of the attic. Bay smiled and turned to the pile of books she had made earlier when she and James had searched for the riddle. My that seemed ages ago!

After some patient searching, Bay selected three books. She wished she could pack them all, but that would be a lot of luggage. Bay carried the books out of the attic and went back to her bedroom. Sitting on the bed Bay cleaned and dusted the books before putting them in her bag. She finished packing when someone knocked at her door and Delon entered.

"Brien is awake," she said, "he wanted to see you." Bay nodded and left her room. Delon went downstairs, and Bay knocked on Brien's door.

"Come in," a weaker version of Brien's voice answered. Bay opened the door. Brien was sitting up in bed, now wearing a shirt over his bandages. The black box containing the typewriter lay on the foot of his bed. Bay smiled warmly at him and sat on a chair by the bed.

"How are you feeling?" Bay asked.

"I've had better, but I have also had worse, so I'm doing pretty good." Bay laughed.

"At least you still have your since of humor," she said.

"Are you all right?" Brien said, "what you did in the cellar was very brave, you saved my life." Bay paused, she had not thought of that. She didn't even realize that, yes she had saved Brien's life. She had been so scared that all she could think about at the time, was getting everyone out of the house.

"I'm fine," Bay said, thinking of the only answer she could give. Brien smiled at her.

"I have something for you," he said. He reached for the bed-side table and picked up a large leather bond notebook. He handed it to Bay, who marveled at it.

"I made that for you, so that you can practice your writing," Brien said. Bay felt a smile form on her face as she flipped through the thick pages, all blank. They seemed to call for the ink of a pen to fill them up. The notebook was made of leather, and a red ribbon was connected on the spine as a bookmark

"Here," Brien handed Bay a small black, ink pen. "It's brand new, and a good quality." Bay beamed and kissed his cheek.

"Thank you Brien!" She said hugging the book to her chest. Brien nodded.

"Go on and finish packing, we leave soon." Bay stood up and left. She carefully put the new notebook in her bag, but stopped. Bay pulled it back out and opened it to the first page. She opened her pen and placed the tip on the paper. She paused for a moment before writing the words: My Adventure, by Bay Paxon. It wasn't a very imaginative title, but it would due for now. Bay sat of the floor with her pen waving across the paper. The words seemed to flow out of her as she wrote the events from the delivery of Brien's suitcase, to now. Soon the world would know about Brien Ink, The Lost Manuscript, and Rivan Hydenburg.

Chapter Nine

Delon made lunch for everybody. Chicken, with corn and potatoes. After they ate Delon wrapped up the leftovers and put them in Brien's bag for the journey. Brien had slept most of the afternoon, but he was soon able to walk around again.

Bay volunteered to load the bags. She took the luggage and stored them on the carriage. James unleashed the horses and gave them a brushing, and a quick walk to warm them up. Once the horses were strapped to the carriage and everything was loaded it was time for good-byes.

Delon teared up, and sniffed, "I hate good-byes," she said giving everyone a hug and kiss.

"It will be all right," Brien assured her, "I will write to you, and we will come visit when this is all over."

"Good luck Brien," Cornelia said, "I may not have been the funniest person to be with, but I always loved you, and you too Bay." Bay smiled and received her first hug from Cornelia. "You are welcomed back anytime," she said.

Brien and Lex got into the drivers seat, while Bay and

James got into the passenger. They waved one last time to Delon and Cornelia. Lex whipped the reins and the horses trotted down the road. Bay looked out the window and watched the two women until they were merely dots in the horizon.

"Do you think we will see them again?" Bay asked bringing her head back into the carriage.

"Of course," James said. Bay leaned back in her seat and looked out at the familiar landscape of Whipshire. She looked at James who was fiddling with something in his pocket.

"James, could you play your harmonica?" Bay asked. James looked at her in mild surprise, then smiled in understanding, and nodded. James pulled the golden harmonica out of his pocket and put it to his lips. The carriage filled with the lovely melody. Bay closed her eyes, so that only the music existed. James played on for a long time, or at least what seemed a long time. When the song was over Bay didn't open her eyes, she let the music echo in her ears for awhile.

"That was beautiful James," she said. James smiled at her.

"Thanks sunshine." James looked out at the landscape then looked back at Bay. "Bay, promise me you will be careful."

"What do you mean?" Bay asked.

"I mean that this will be a dangerous adventure, it's not like your books. I would be devastated if anything happened to you, and I can't always protect you, so promise me you will be careful." Bay stared at him then nodded.

"I promise." James smiled then placed the harmonica back to his lips, and played. Half and hour later Lex stopped the carriage in front of the train station. Bay had never ridden a train, her heart was beating with excitement as they entered the station. People hurried past them trying to get to the train, or to the loved ones waiting for them. Bay grabbed her father's hand so that they wouldn't get separated.

Lex and Brien both chipped in some money to pay for the tickets. The train was early so they boarded and quickly found seats where they could sit together.

Bay looked around at the long cars with amazement. The seats were tall and cushioned, and they were gathered in pairs of four with seats facing each other. Bay sat by the window with Lex next to her, and Brien and James across from them.

Steam from the train rolled past the window making it difficult to see. Bay studied the platform and the people then leaned back impatiently in her seat waiting for the train to move.

"How much longer?" Bay asked. Lex looked at his pocket watch.

"Just a few more minutes. Be patient." Bay reached into her carry-on bag and pulled out a book. She read on for awhile, when a sudden jerk brought her out of the fantasy world. Bay looked up in surprise and saw that the train was beginning to move. It rolled slowly, gaining speed as it went.

Bay looked out the window eagerly watching the platform move away, and the English countryside fill up the site. The train went faster and faster, until the world was simply a blur of color and light. Bay leaned back in her chair and pulled out the Train Heist book, she had reached the part where Richard Calle was boarding the train he planned to rob.

The minutes turned to hours, and they past by at a steady slowness. James fell asleep, Brien pulled out his notebook to write, and Lex read to himself. It was three o'clock when Bay finished her book and put it away. She looked around at the car they were in. There were not many people with them. A tall man sat in the far corner by the door, his face hidden behind a newspaper. An elderly woman sat across the isle from them, her small glasses slid down her nose as she read the book in her hands. Behind them were a newly married couple on their way to the honeymoon, and finally in the back of the car were two men dressed in business suits talking to each other quietly.

Bay's stomach let out a low grumble of hunger. It was just the right time for an early supper. "Dad?" Bay whispered, it was so quiet in the car she was to scared to speak loudly. Lex glanced up from his book.

"I'm hungry, is there any chicken left in the bag?" Lex thought to himself for a moment then reached into his pocket and revealed some money.

"Since this is your first train ride, you can get something from the club car." Bay smiled and gratefully took the money. "It's two cars ahead of us," Lex explained, "you have to jump between the cars to get there. The tracks are dangerous, so be careful." Bay nodded eagerly and stood up. She walked down the isle quietly, so as not to disturb the other passengers. When she reached the door, the man with the newspaper glanced at her, but said nothing.

Bay opened the door and stepped out onto the railing. The wind whipped around her, slapping her face, and the noise of the powerful wheels filled her ears. Bay looked down, the cars were connected by a very thick metal latch, and bolt. Under that you could see the blur of the train tracks. Very carefully, Bay placed her foot on the latch and with a quick leap she jumped the space between the two cars, and landed safely on the opposite railing.

For only a brief moment Bay imagined herself slipping on the rail and falling under the train, being sucked onto the tracks. But this thought disappeared quickly, like a car passing you in the next lane, and Bay entered the next car.

This was identical to her car, except for the fact that there were more people there. Some glanced up briefly to see who had entered their car, then went back to what they were doing. Bay made her way swiftly down the isle, she was eager to try jumping the cars again. Bay opened the door at the end of the car and stepped out onto the railing.

This time Bay didn't put her foot on the latch, with a deep breath she leaped and landed on the second rail. It felt as though she had flown, only for a second. Bay laughed to herself and entered the car.

This was the club car. Tables lined on wall, while a long bar filled up the other. Two other people were sitting at the tables eating quietly. Behind the bar and man sat on a stool polishing glasses, as if it were a fine art.

Bay approached the bar carefully. She didn't eat out often, and was unsure how to order her food. But the man at the bar seemed to since her uneasiness. He looked up and grinned at her.

"Your first train ride?" He asked. Bay's eyes widened in

surprise, and she nodded. "You jump those cars good for a first timer," the man said. Bay blushed a little and smiled. "What can I get you?" Bay studied the menu written over the bar, it was mostly sandwiches, and drinks. Bay counted out her money and added up the price.

"Could I have a ham sandwich and a soda please?"

"You most certainly can." The man spun around. His quick hands made a tall glass of soda, and a club sandwich in a matter of minutes. Bay paid then sat at a table. The sandwich was delicious, and the soda popped and frizzed in her mouth. Bay ate it all until she was content. She threw away the trash and was about to leave when the man at the bar beckoned her to come back. He reached into his pocket and pulled out a small, wrapped, chocolate bar and handed it to her.

"That should give you enough energy to jump the cars," he said smiling, "on the house." Bay beamed and put the chocolate in her pocket.

"Thank you!" she said. The man nodded to her. Bay turned to leave, and ran into someone's chest. "Oh! Sorry, I...." Bay stopped mid-sentence, her mouth dropped in horror as she stared up into Rivan's cold eyes.

"Hello Bay. We keep running into each other don't we?" Rivan said this casually, as if they were old friends. Rivan grabbed her arm and gripped it tightly, Bay was too shocked to pull away. "Let's go see if we can find Brien," Rivan said. He began leading her away from the bar. Bay's mind panicked. She quickly looked behind her and stared at the man behind the bar. He winked at her.

That wink seemed to send a shock through her body, and Bay controlled her own thoughts. With a gasp, she brought her foot up and kicked Rivan in the stomach. Rivan winced, but he didn't release his hold on her arm. Bay opened her mouth and sank her teeth into Rivan's hand. Rivan gasped and let go. Bay ran down the isle as fast as she could towards the door. Rivan was right behind her.

Bay opened the door and jumped the railing without

thinking about it. But as she started to open the second door a man appeared blocking her way. Bay immediately recognized Red. His hair was burnt off, and Bay could smell burnt flesh about him, but he was still alive, and hungry for revenge. There was only one place to go now.

Up.

Bay grabbed the ladder, beside the door and climbed up faster than a squirrel. Red tried to grab her leg, but he missed. Bay heard Rivan order, "I've got her, go back inside. Watch the car."

Bay crawled out on top of the car. It was flat and slick. The edges slopped just a little bit. One wrong move would send you over the edge. The strong wind whipped her hair, and steam from the engine blinded her. The train jerked so roughly Bay thought she would fall.

Rivan climbed up behind her, he remained balanced on the car. Bay stood up on trembling legs, and carefully stepped away from him.

"Give it up!" Rivan yelled over the wind, "If you try to run, or struggle, you will send us both over the edge!" At least I can take you with me, Bay thought. Rivan walked toward her, but Bay moved away from him. James was right, this wasn't like a book. In the book about the train heist, Richard had walked on top of the cars to get to the one car that held the gold. It was much easier reading about it than actually doing it though. Bay felt she might fall off any minute, but she had to push this fear away. Rivan was getting closer, she couldn't afford to be slow.

Bay turned and made her way across the car, trying to be careful, but fast as well. Rivan was right behind her, he too was being careful, in his mind he knew he had Bay trapped, there was no need to get excited and fall off the train.

Bay was almost to the end. If she could get there she could get back inside the car. Brien and Lex were just in front of her. Bay glanced behind to see how close Rivan was, he was still a few feet away, but that wasn't what got her attention. In the distance, but gaining space, was a low bridge.

Bay gasped and dropped to her stomach. Rivan turned and saw the bridge as well. He ducked down, if he had been any later the bridge would have knocked him off. Bay felt the whoosh! and brief moment of darkness as they past under it. Once they had though, both Rivan and Bay jumped up and Rivan advanced on her.

Bay turned and jogged the rest of the way to the end of the car, feeling too frightened to be careful. Bay got on her knees and was about to climb down the ladder when she saw a face appear in the window of the opposite car. It was Cue, the man with the newspaper, Bay had not recognized him with a hat on.

She was trapped. With Cue in one car, Red in the other, and Rivan right behind her, there was no where to go. Unless she took a leaf from the train heist book. In the book the ladder on the last car was broken off, to get to the car Richard had jumped the space between them. Bay studied the air between the cars, it wasn't very big, but it was a moving train, if she missed, the only thing to catch her was the ground at fifty miles a hour.

Rivan was right behind her now. Bay sucked in her breath and took a step back, for a running start. Rivan seemed to since what she was going to do.

"Don't try it kid!" He yelled, "you'll get yourself killed!" Rivan lunged for her. Bay ran out of his way, and leaped.

Bay felt nothing but air around her for a few seconds. Her legs were spread out like a ballerina. Bay felt her heart stop in fear for that short jump. She landed on the second car, her feet slipped out from under her on the slick metal and Bay felt herself slid toward the edge.

Bay screamed, her hands shot out looking for anything to grab. Her fingers wrapped themselves tightly around a thin bar railing on the edge of the roof, and hung on for dear life.

The wind made Bay float a few inches as she dangled like a worm on a hook over the train's edge, the ground flew by dangerously. Bay screamed out in fear, she managed to look up and see Rivan quickly making his way down the ladder to the railing.

Bay dangled in front of a window. The seat inside was empty, but in the seat in front of it was the older woman still reading her book. Bay took a deep breath, and made a quick prayer. She slip her hand down the bar slowly moving her body forward closer to the window.

Her heart pounded in her ears, and her stomach was an empty pit. Wind blew all around her whipping her face with her blond hair, making it difficult to see. Bay's arms trembled with fear and the effort to hold her body. Bay continued to make her way to the next window. Rivan was climbing up the ladder once again to reach her. Bay stopped in front of the woman's window. Her arms ached, but she ignored it. Bay brought her foot up and kicked the window as hard as she could with her knee. It wasn't very loud, but it was enough to get the woman's attention.

She looked up from her book to see what had made the noise. When she saw the little girl hanging off the edge of the train she screamed in fear and surprise.

"HELP ME!" Bay screamed with all her might. The woman opened the window, and Bay spotted Lex, Brien and James across the isle.

"DADDY!" Bay screamed again. Lex looked up in horror and screamed. He jumped up and ran to the window, Brien followed. Behind them James had woken up and was looking around with confusion.

"Hang on Bay, I've got you!" Lex reached his hands out the window to grab her, but Rivan had reached her first. Bay felt his large hands wrap around her wrist and began pulling her up.

"Dad help!" Bay screamed as Rivan pulled her back onto the roof. Bay was too tired and too scared to fight back. Rivan grabbed her and began to lead her back to the ladder.

Inside the car Brien was being held back by Cue. Cue punched him in the face, and Brien felt blood run out of his lip. Lex came from behind him and jumped on Cue. The two men fell to the ground and struggled fiercely.

"Help Bay!" Lex managed to scream at Brien, before Cue punched him again. Brien jumped over the two men and opened the door to the railing. He climbed up the ladder to the top, where Rivan held Bay tightly. Her face was white with fear, and her entire body trembled. Brien glared at Rivan and advanced toward him.

Rivan pulled out a knife, Brien stopped before he could place it to Bay's delicate throat.

"She stays with me Brien, and you take me to the manuscript." Rivan said. Brien felt nausea fill his stomach.

"Please Rivan, let her go. This is between you and me." Rivan grinned and shook his head.

"Don't worry I'll make sure she is safe. As long as you do as I say."

"Fine I'll do what ever you want," Brien said.

"Good. Now, we are going to get back in the car. Bay here was just playing on top of the car and slipped off, you and I rescued her, no harm done. We will sit together the rest of the trip and you will lead us to the manuscript. My associate, Jacob, will be the young lady's bodyguard, understand?" Brien nodded. "Good, let's go."

Still holding Bay, Rivan followed Brien back down the ladder into the car. Lex and Cue had stopped the fight. Cue lay on the ground looking dazed. Lex was nursing his bad arm.

When they entered, Lex jumped up, but Rivan showed him the knife, and he did not attack. Bay pulled forward and Rivan released her. Bay ran to Lex who held her in his arms tightly.

"My God, are you okay?" Lex whispered. Bay didn't answer, she simply hugged him tighter.

"Just fine, right Brien?" Rivan asked.

"Yeah," Brien said forcefully, "She was just playing on top of the cars, that's it." Lex stared at Brien in horror, but Brien whispered, "trust me," in his ear. Lex nodded and sat down. Bay huddled close to him when Red entered, though his real name was apparently Jacob.

Red sat down by Bay and Lex, Rivan sat by Brien and James, who glared at him. Cue managed to sit up and lay down on an empty seat.

"What is going on?" The woman with the book stood in front of them, like a teacher scolding her students.

"It's fine now ma'am," Rivan said, "there was an accident on top of the train, but the little lady is fine, right sweetheart?" Bay hid her face in Lex's jacket. Lex put a protected arm around her and whispered in her ear. "Be strong Bay."

"Why were these men fighting like a bunch of wild dogs?" the woman demanded.

"An old family grudge," Lex said looking at Cue. The woman stared at them for a while, she didn't believe a word they said, and Brien knew it, but she went back to her seat, and pretended to read, but her eyes kept wondering away from the pages, back to them.

Gradually, Bay's courage, and will came back. She sat up and gripped Lex's hand tightly. Brien winked confidently at her, and Bay wondered what was going on in that interesting mind of his. James looked at her with concern for awhile, then his gaze went to Jacob, and James watched him like a hawk the entire trip.

The train stopped at Portville England. The small city bordered the English channel, it was here that people could board a ferry and sail on to France. The group of seven left the train together. They grabbed the bags and walked out into the station. Jacob held Bay's arm. But Lex never left her side. They left the station and hailed a cab. The seven of them managed to squeeze into the car together, and drove to the channel.

They ferry planned on leaving in less than half a hour. The port was busy with the crowd of people trying to get on the ferry before it ran out of room. Bay held Lex's hand so she wouldn't get lost. She tried to loose Jacob, but he stuck very close. Bay noticed that James always kept two steps behind Jacob, she could tell by the look in his eye that he had something planned.

Brien and Rivan walked together as if to keep an eye on each other. Seeing them together, two enemies walking side by side, it gave Bay a feeling of discomfort, and uneasiness. She wished they would separate.

Everyone boarded the ferry. Like the train, Bay had never been on one. She looked over the railing down at the water. Seagulls flew around the boat making that annoying noise. People watched the birds and threw bread to them. The seagulls would swoop down and catch it in midair, and some even dived into the water to get the bread. Bay couldn't help but smile at them, for a split moment she forgot they were hostages.

They crowded into a corner together. Bay watched the other people walking around on the platform, talking, laughing, and throwing bread. Bay wanted to join them, but she glanced at Rivan and her hopes seemed to disappear.

A man suddenly shouted, "cast off!" The ferry gave a jerk and slowly began it's sail to the French shore. Bay felt a since of excitement, for this would be the first time she had ever left England.

People waved to their loved ones still on the shore. Women threw out flowers that landed on the water. Bay watched the colorful petals float out on the water, and she smiled. It wasn't over yet, Rivan had not won yet.

Bay stared down at the water, watching it lap around the ferry peacefully. James came up beside her and touched her waist, he leaned forward until his lips were brushing her ear.

"Do you trust me Bay?"

"Of course I do," Bay whispered back, she didn't look at him in case Jacob, or Rivan were looking, "You know I do James."

"Yes, I just wanted to hear you say it. I'll see you Bay."

"What do you mean?" Bay asked. This time she looked up into his pretty, hazel eyes. James winked. He placed his foot on the rail and jumped into the water.

"James!" Bay called out to him, but there was only a splash, and he was gone. The others came up beside her and peered into the water, but it was still, James was no where to be seen.

"Looks like your friend decided to bail out," Rivan said with a satisfied smile. Bay wanted to slap him, and make that awful smile disappear, but she held back. Lex and Brien glanced at Bay. She quickly gave them a wink to show that James was all right.

Bay stood at the railing for the rest of the trip. The French shore line soon appeared in the distance. Bay would look around the ferry once in awhile trying to find James, but he was no where in site.

The five men stood in the corner quietly. Bay felt alone, her father was here yes, but James was closer to her age, for some reason this made her feel more comfortable. Bay managed to get some space between herself and Jacob. Rivan had sent Cue to look around the ferry in case James had faked his escape.

As Bay stood there bending over the railing watching the water, a young boy suddenly appeared at her side. He had very messy hair, wide blue eyes and a goofy smile.

His appearance made Bay look twice, she couldn't help but take a step back, he seemed to be full of energy that overflowed and shocked other people. He gave her one of his goofy smiles.

"Did you see that guy who jumped off the ferry? That happens sometimes, people will pay for a ferry ride then jump off halfway to swim back, it's kind of funny sometimes." Bay stared at him with wide eyes, unsure of what to say. She glanced over at the others. Jacob was watching her with some amusement. The others hadn't seen yet, but it was only a matter of time, and Bay did not want Rivan and his henchmen watch her in her social life.

"Um, yeah, a little funny," Bay said. She tried to move away from the strange boy, but he simply followed her like a puppy that had gotten a snack.

"My father is captain of the ferry," the boy said, "so I see a lot of stuff happen. I can even name out the seagulls, I recognize them. That one there, with the brown stripe on his back is Leroy, and that one with the bread is Bumpy."

"Bumpy?" Bay asked.

"He bumps into the window all the time, he can never learn that there is a glass between him and the control room." Bay chuckled a little. She looked over at the men again. This time Lex was watching her with a father's interest, and Rivan was giving her an evil, teasing smile. Bay felt herself blush, and she glared at him. Rivan smirked.

"Are you with them?" the boy asked.

"Something like that," Bay said.

"A lucky girl with five men, looks like I've got my work cut out for me." Bay blushed deeper. Rivan said something snide to Lex. Lex didn't answer, he continued to watch Bay. Brien just now noticed that she had found a friend. Brien winked.

"I'm not lucky," Bay said.

"What do you mean?" The boy suddenly became serious. Bay mustered up a smile to make them think that the conversation was anything but serious.

"Three of those men have kidnapped my father, his friend, and me. They are taking us to France, and are using me as leverage." The boy stared at Bay for a while, Bay looked him in the eye.

"You are serious," the boy said. Bay nodded. "I can tell my dad, he is the captain, we can turn the ferry around and call the police," the boy offered.

"This is different than ordinary kidnappings, police can't stop these men, but you can help us get away," Bay said. The boy's face brightened.

"What can I do?"

"Tell your father that those men are doing something illegal, I don't care what. When the ferry stops hold them back long enough for us to make our escape."

"Consider it done. Though you will owe me a date for giving my dad false alarms."

"If this works I owe you more than a date," Bay promised.

105

The boy smiled and winked, "by the way my name is Joey."

"I'm Bay." Joey grinned then he was gone. Bay hoped he would be true to his word. Bay turned and quietly made her way back to Lex. Rivan continued to give her that mean, teasing grin. Bay looked away from him.

"Who was that?" Lex whispered in her ear.

"Just a little boy looking for attention," Bay said. She didn't like lying to her father, but how could she tell him anything in front of Rivan? Jacob moved closer to them, to make sure Bay didn't wander off again.

Bay glanced up at the control room of the ferry once in awhile to see if Joey had done what she asked. But it was hard to see anything through the window. Bay turned and looked at the nearing shore line instead.

Lex seemed to become more and more anxious the closer they got. He stroked Bay's hair, then simply wrapped an arm around her shoulders. Bay looked up an smiled at him, to show that she was not afraid.

The ferry finally docked on the coast. While people hustled to get off, the group held back.

"No tricks now," Rivan said to Brien and Lex, "and don't try to run, we would hate for Jacob to scar up her pretty face." Rivan stroked Bay's cheek. Bay jerked back and slapped his hand away, glaring at him hotly, Rivan only chuckled.

Jacob gripped Bay's arm and they started weaving their way through the crowd to get off the ferry. Bay looked around, feeling desperate, where was Joey? They had almost reached the platform, it would soon be to late.

Suddenly two men in uniforms appeared. One grabbed Rivan's arm and pulled him back. Cue and Jacob stopped as well.

"Excuse me sir, I'm going to have to check your bag before you leave," one of the uniforms said. Bay knew this was her chance. With a strong jerk she pulled out of Jacob's grasp. Lex held her hand and he and Brien led her off the ferry.

106

"Wait! I'm with them!" Rivan said pointing at them. Brien turned and gave the officers a confused look that said, 'I have never seen that man before.'

"You can meet up later," the officer said, "let me see your bag." Joey appeared in the crowd. He waved at Bay and gave her the thumbs up. Bay beamed at him and blew a kiss. Joey blushed then disappeared.

Bay followed Lex and Brien off the ferry onto the dock. They carried their bags to the street where Brien hailed a cab. Bay turned her head and saw Rivan pushing through the crowd looking for them.

"He's coming!" Bay warned. The three of them quickly got into the cab and it drove off down the street. Bay looked out the window, but didn't see Rivan. She sighed with relief and leaned back in the seat.

"That was a lucky break," Lex said.

"It wasn't lucky," Bay corrected him, "that boy I was talking to on the ferry, he is the captain's son. I told him what happened and he gave the guards a false alarm."

"Well done Bay!" Brien said, "you have a very extraordinary daughter Lex."

"She gets it from her mother," Lex said. Bay smiled a little, she missed her mom, even though she couldn't remember her very well. She had died of cancer when Bay was two years old. It didn't hurt her like it hurt Lex.

Everyone was silent in the cab for the rest of the trip. Brien hummed a song, but that was it. Bay looked out the window at the country of France. It was like England, except it was a little more dirty, and everything was written in French. Bay studied to tall buildings, and the people with their strange clothing. She couldn't help but smile at the differences between the two countries.

The cab stopped in front of a short building and they unboarded the cab. Bay stared up at the strange writing trying to figure out where they were.

"What is this place Brien?" Bay asked as she picked up her bag and entered the building.

"It's a train station, it will take us straight to Germany. There we will buy a horse and buggy and go on to Shireville."

"You still want to go there?" Bay asked, "I think we should go to the manuscript. If Rivan catches us again it won't be easy getting away."

"Trust me on this Bay, we need to go to Shireville," Brien said. Bay didn't answer. They entered the train station and bought tickets for the five o'clock to Germany.

"How many languages can you speak?" Bay asked as they boarded the train. When they did Bay felt a since of fear, but she grabbed Lex's hand and tried to ignore it.

"French, German, Italian, Swedish, and a few others. I'm not very fluent, but it's enough." They sat at a chair, and the same fear crept into Bay's thoughts again. She glanced up at the ceiling, then out the window at the bar on the edge of the train. She shuddered. Lex put an arm around her.

"It's okay Bay, nothing bad will happen this time, I promise." Lex dug through his bag and pulled out the leftovers Delon had packed them, he slapped some chicken on bread and handed it to Bay. She managed to eat a little, but the bird seemed tasteless. She forced it down and curled up on the soft chair. Her eyes closed, and she was asleep before the train jerked to life and began it's journey.

Chapter Ten

Lex had to shake Bay awake when the train stopped in Germany later that night. He wanted to let her sleep on, but he couldn't carry her, he was very tired himself. The three of them left the station quietly, Bay was only half awake. Lex kept his arm around her in case she fell asleep while walking.

They found a small, cheap Inn down the street. It was small, dirty, and run down, but it was still cheap. Brien paid the bill. Bay noticed that he always had cash on hand, and she wondered where it came from. Bay stumbled sleepily on the stairs. Brien picked her up, and carried her the rest of the way, she fell asleep in his arms. It was very late. Lex took their bags and they made their way up the stairs into a small bedroom. There were two beds and a dresser in the corner. The ceiling was cracked like a piece of ancient pottery, and the furniture was old and falling apart. Brien put Bay down on the bed and took off her shoes. The thin mattress sagged under their weight, the place was a little better than a workhouse, but it was better than the streets, so they turned in for the night, which had already proved long. Lex yawned, he set down the bags and took off his shoes and shirt.

Brien stood up and locked the door and closed the curtains. Lex pulled up the covers and got on the bed beside Bay. She stirred in her sleep, but didn't wake. Lex played with a strand of golden hair. Brien got in the second bed and laid his head on the scratchy pillow. He was a light sleeper, but he felt very tired tonight. Though his mind was too restless to sleep. His mind drifted all over the place, he worried about James, and he wondered where Rivan was, he couldn't be too far behind them, in fact he may have followed them here like he followed them on the train.

Brien looked at the other bed. Lex was sitting up. Bay had her head on top of his chest, she slept peacefully. Lex had his hand on her head, neither could sleep for the same reasons.

"I'm sorry Lex," Brien whispered. Lex looked at him solemnly.

"There is nothing to apologize for Brien, I came with you willingly. So did Bay, she wanted to come, she wanted to have an adventure." Lex looked down at her and sighed sadly, "it killed me every time I had to leave her on the farm, she deserved better than that, she has to much spirit in her to hide away."

Brien nodded in agreement, "she is like her mother," he said. Lex smiled. Brien remembered how Lex looked at his wife the same way he looked at Bay.

Time dragged by slowly, Lex finally fell into a light, fitful sleep, but Brien remained awake. He fell into the abyss of his thoughts, he wanted to leave. He could go on to Shireville himself, then Lex and Bay would be out of danger. No, they would not be out of danger, Rivan would capture them and use them as bait to get Brien, they were not safe, but they were together, that was better than nothing.

By midnight Brien knew he was not going to sleep that night. He got out of bed and went to the bags. He pulled out the box that Delon had given him and opened the lid. He smiled down at the typewriter like an old friend. This was the typewriter where he had learned to type, and write full length stories.

Brien found a lovely blank sheet of paper in his bag and put it into the typewriter. His fingers flowed across the keys, their loud clicks filled up the room, but did not wake Lex or Bay. The hours past on but Brien didn't stop, nor did he feel the effects of the sleepless night. It was time to bring the right story into the lost manuscript.

***

Lex and Bay woke up early the next morning, before the sun had risen into the sky. Brien was lying on his bed on top of the covers. His typewriter sat on the corner of the bed, and a small stack of papers lay below it on the floor. Some where crumpled and tossed into a corner, but the finished story was there all the same.

Bay picked up the story while Lex packed anything from the night before. Bay soon discovered that this was Rivan's story, the true one, not the one of his ghost father. Brien had written it last night, now it was ready to be put into The Lost Manuscript.

When Brien woke they left the Inn and had breakfast in a small coffee shop. Brien and Lex forked some money and bought a small buggy. It was old and falling apart, but it was all they could afford. They also purchased a horse to pull it. He was a dirty gray, and sickly looking, Brien named him Seabiscut.

"What's a Seabiscut?" Bay asked as they boarded the buggy.

"He is a famous horse in America, he is just a small sickly thing, but he has won every race, and has even beaten the strongest, largest, and fastest horse in the racing world." Bay looked at the gray Seabiscut and laughed out loud.

"Well, this fellow may not when any races, but he has a lot of heart, so let's get going," Brien said. He whipped the reins and Seabiscut rode forward down the road towards Shireville.

"How far is Shireville?" Bay asked.

"A little ways, but we should get there by supper time," Brien said.

"Do you think James is okay?" Bay asked.

"If I know James he will be at the village before we are," Brien said. There was so much confidence in his voice that Bay felt the worry in her heart melt away. Of course James was fine! Rivan didn't have him, James had left the ferry to get help, and he would see them in Shireville. Bay sighed and leaned back in her seat.

The German country side was nice, Bay felt a little nervous, for she remembered stories of the first war. But the country seemed peaceful now, farmers tended their gardens, older folks sat on the porches, and children played in the fields.

The three of them talked about things that were not important to anybody but them, when they ran out of things to talk about they read books, and when they got tired of reading, they played those little games that get boring quickly, the ones you play when you are bored and trapped inside a car, or in this case a buggy.

"I spy something that looks small, but is actually huge. Up, up it goes, but it never grows," Brien loved riddles and he thought up some great ones for Lex and Bay to guess at. Eager to outwit him Bay and Lex also tried to think up riddles that he had no answer too.

"It's the mountains in the distance!" Lex said pointing at the small slopes in the horizon.

"I spy something that you cannot see, it whispers but has no mouth, it fly's but has no wings, what is it?" Bay asked. A long thoughtful silence followed. Bay smiled at the confused looks on their faces. For a moment she believed that she had won but Brien snapped his fingers.

"Of course, it's the wind!" he said. Bay bowed her head and nodded. "Don't worry about it little one, there are many who are better than riddles than I am, you will think of one I cannot solve."

But they soon grew tired of the game, and all was silent. A small town loomed into view.

"Is that Shireville?" Bay asked hopefully.

"No, Shireville is in the next town. We can get some lunch here and move on." Brien gave the reins another whip. Seabiscut speeded his pace and they entered the small German town.

It was quaint, it reminded Bay of Whipshire, but it had a different tone to it, like two blocks of wood, they are the same size and quality, but when you hit them with a stick there is a different sound, this was like the German version of Whipshire.

It was a small town. When the three strangers rode into town on the worn buggy everyone looked up from their work. Inn keepers eagerly awaited in their buildings, and a stable master came out and offered to brush the horse and fix the buggy.

"Nice German hospitality," Bay said when Brien translated their words.

"Small towns usually have kind moods," Lex said. They stopped the buggy and let the stable master do his work. While they waited they found a restaurant to eat lunch.

They sat in a corner and ate quietly. Bay enjoyed the meal, it was nice to eat at a place where you didn't cook the meals, and you could have almost what ever you asked for. They were quiet for awhile, somewhere inside they felt that if they talked Rivan would hear them. But the mood soon lightened and they were talking and laughing like normal folks who were not being chased by desperate criminals.

Everyone helped themselves to hardy meals, and Lex even got Bay an ice cream for desert. When it was done they leaned back into their chairs, full stomachs, and content minds. Bay stood up and found a bathroom in the back of the restaurant.

Bay washed her hands, and combed her hair with her fingers. She stared at the face in the mirror that was hers. Long blond hair past her shoulders, and pretty blue eyes. Bay pulled her hair into a ponytail, and straightened her clothes. Oh well, Bay thought to herself, I'm not the most beautiful girl in the world, but it could be worse. Bay smiled, she didn't care how she looked, she was happy and healthy.

Bay turned and walked out of the bathroom. In the corner of her eye she only saw a shadow, it darted toward her quickly and grabbed her. Before Bay could scream for help, a large hand covered her mouth and a muscular arm wrapped itself around her arms. The figure pulled her back into a dark corner where no one could see.

Bay struggled helplessly, but the man was very strong. "Time for payback," the voice whispered in her ear. He spoke English, but he had a heavy German accent. Bay let out a muffled yell and pulled forward, but the man only held her tighter. Bay felt a cold metal on her neck, her body froze in terror as the knife ran down her skin onto her chest, her heart felt as though it would explode, and small drops of sweat formed on her forehead.

"Brien Ink is a hard man to find, but I knew we would run into each other someday." This wasn't Rivan. Bay thought of the murderer Brien had told her about, and the secrets he had reveled about them, what would he do?

The man simply stood there clutching Bay tightly. Bay struggled, but he pressed the knife to her throat, and she remained still. A few minutes went by, at the table Lex kept glancing at the rest room door wondering what was keeping Bay.

"I'm going to go check on her," Lex said.

"I'll join you," Brien offered, they left a bill on the table and went to the rest rooms. They turned the corner and saw a tall beefy man holding Bay. When the man saw them turn the corner he immediately let go of the girl, but he pointed the knife at Brien.

Bay ran to her father. Lex put a protective arm around her. The man shook his knife at Brien, his eyes filled with anger.

"You have a lot of nerve coming back here Ink, or maybe your just stupid."

"You know me better than that Darc," Brien said, his voice was solemn, and a little sarcastic, "Why did you have to go and scare Bay like that?" Brien took a threatening step forward, and Bay saw something like fear in Darc's eyes.

"You know I don't hurt people Ink," Darc said, "I just needed to get your attention." Brien tapped his foot on the ground and stared at Darc coldly.

"You stay away from my friends," Brien said.

"Don't talk to me like that Ink, you owe me, and this time I'm not letting you leave town."

"Brien what's going on?" Lex demanded, "who is this?"

"We need to go someplace more private," Brien said.

"Fine," Darc pushed past them and walked out into the restaurant.

"You can come if you want," Brien told Lex. Lex nodded he took Bay's hand and they followed Darc to a room in the back of the restaurant. Boxes were stacked up against the walls, and a few other storage items. They all sat on some boxes circling each other, Bay felt like they were kids around a campfire ready for story time. Brien gave the first one.

"This is Stanley Darc," Brien said, "I met him here a few years ago. When I escaped Rivan the night he tortured me, Darc found me on the road when he was riding by, he took me to a hospital, then let me stay in his house. But that night Rivan came again, he had followed us to the house."

"They stole my money, and cut off my ear!" Darc finished for him. Darc removed his hat and Bay gasped when she saw the stub that was once his ear. Darc replaced his hat, hiding the deformed ear.

"I am sorry about that Darc," Brien said, "but I don't see how I can pay you back for that, I have some money."

"I don't want money," Darc said, "I want the man who cut off my ear, I want him in jail, or dead."

"So do I Darc," Brien said.

"Then he is still after you!" Darc snapped, "you led him back here, didn't you?"

"Yes Darc he is following me, I don't know if he's here or not."

"Why did you come back?"

"Because I knew you would want revenge on Rivan, if you want him in jail, this could be your chance." Darc held up a thick finger and pointed it at him.

"I'm not risking my hide to save you again," Darc said, "I have a family to look after."

"I know that," Brien said, "I'm not asking you to risk much, I just need you to set a trap for Rivan."

"And what kind of trap would that be?" Darc asked.

"We are leaving later today," Brien said, "but Rivan could

be right behind us, if he is you can use my plan to put him in jail, this should satisfy your need for revenge, and give us a few days head start." Darc nodded his head thoughtfully, then let out a loud laugh, it made Bay jump in surprise. Darc's laugh was loud and sudden, like a firework.

"I don't know what it is about you Ink, one moment your my worse enemy, the next we are like old friends in a pub. What's your little plan then?" Brien smiled and sat up.

"When Rivan shows up I want you to make him believe that we are staying in your house. Get your family out of course, but when he comes in to find us you call the police and they catch him 'robbing' your house, get it?"

Darc laughed again, "that should get him in jail for a few weeks!" he exclaimed, "fine Ink, I'll get the bastard in jail. But, I don't want to see your face in this town again, got it?"

"Your not the sheriff Darc, and I won't make any promises I can't keep," Brien said. They all stood up and left the musty storage room.

"Fine, get out of here," Darc said, not unkindly. The trio turned and started to leave when Darc called them back.

"Ink! Good luck with your book, I hope you get it published." Brien nodded to him and they left the shop. It was past the hour of two when they loaded the buggy with fresh supplies and started off again. Bay felt sleepy from the long ride, and the meal. She curled up in the back of the buggy and pulled out a blanket from the bag. She fell asleep with the fresh scent of country air in her noise, and a since of security in her mind.

Chapter Eleven

The sun was setting in the distance when Bay awoke. Brien was sleeping beside her, with Lex in the front. Bay crawled into the seat next to him, careful as to not disturb Brien.

"He must have been up all night writing that story," Lex said, "He never liked sleeping, he said to took to much time off his life, time when he could be writing." Bay laughed.

"He is strange sometimes," Bay said.

"You have no idea." Lex yawned in boredom, Seabiscut also looked tired and worn out. More than usual anyway. Bay strained her eyes, she spotted some smoke rising in the air, and the tops of buildings in the distance.

"Chimney smoke," Lex said, "that must be Shireville."

"Good," Bay said, "I feel like we've been riding in this buggy forever." Lex chuckled and kissed her cheek.

"Things are going to be different from now on Bay," he said. Bay looked at him with concern, she had never welcomed change, it didn't always turn out the way you intended.

"What do you mean?" She asked.

"Well, when Brien gets his book published we won't be on the run. I'm going to quit my job as a delivery man. I want to stay home, and spend more time with you."

"We still have to make money," Bay protested.

"Don't worry, I can get a new job, one that's close to home," Lex said. Bay smiled and laid her head on his chest.

"Will this have a happy ending dad?"

"I can't guarantee happy endings darling. But things always work out in the end, somehow." Bay sighed and watched as the town of Shireville came closer. The top of the sun, and the different colors filled up the sky like a beautiful painting when they entered Shireville.

It was an old village, the streets were made of bricks, and cobble stones. The houses and shops were made of stone and old wood. The largest building was the Catholic church, made of stone, with lovely statues watching them from the lawn. Bay loved the town instantly, it was peaceful, and lovely, like an antique store. Bay woke Brien. He opened his eyes with alarm, but calmed when he saw where they were. He got in the seat with them and gave Lex directions to an Inn.

The streets were mostly empty, only a few people were out, everyone else had closed their shops and had gone home to a warm house and a hot supper. It was called Shireville Inn, it was a modest place, small, but by no means uncomfortable. A small, slightly overweight woman ran the Inn, she was cheerful, and overly optimistic to the point where she could see the bright side of a train wreck.

She greeted Brien as if he were her long lost son. She hugged him tightly and kissed his cheek, leaving a lipstick mark behind.

"Everyone, this is Mallory Giono," Brien said introducing them, "Mallory, this is

my friend Lex, and his daughter Bay Paxon."

"Hello!" Mallory greeted them, "Any friend of Brien's is welcome. You must be tired from your trip, I'm just making supper, come in!" Bay could almost feel the energy coming off of Mallory, she smiled and helped her father carry the bags inside the Inn.

They entered a cozy living room. A large fire burned

brightly, cushioned chairs and couches were spread out around the room. Against the walls were two bookshelves piled high with books. The room was decorated mostly with flowers sitting on the coffee table, and fireplace mantle. Lovely watercolor paintings were hung all over the walls, they were mostly flowers, and pictures of the country side.

Mallory gave Brien a key, "You can have your old room," Mallory said, "I've missed you and that continuous typewriter," she said. Mallory got a far away look in her eye and wandered off into the kitchen. Lex and Bay followed Brien up a flight of stairs to the room. It was also small and cozy like most of the Inn. There were two beds piled with thick blankets and fluffy pillows. There was a tall dresser and mirror, and even a desk in the corner. Bay set the bags down and yawned. She sat down on the soft bed and stretched.

"You can't go to sleep yet," Brien said, "not until you have supper, and believe me, Mallory is an excellent cook." Bay sniffed the air, she could smell chicken and potatoes drifting from downstairs, and her stomach gave a soft grumble.

"How do you know Mallory?" Bay asked as she changed her shoes.

"I actually lived in Shireville for a few weeks before I met Rivan. I had been traveling for quite awhile, so I stopped here one day, rented a room and just stayed. I spent most of the time resting and typing up the manuscript. I stayed so long Mallory and I just sort of grew on each other. Then one night Mallory got invited to a small get-together, she brought me along. That was when I heard Rivan's story, when they had storytelling, I became very interested and asked a lot of questions, to many questions I guess because that night Rivan came to my room."

Bay knew the rest. The three of them washed up then followed Brien to the dinning room. The food and plates were all ready set out, there was chicken, and baked potatoes, along with green beans, bread rolls, and corn. Also a chocolate cake for dessert.

Bay sat down eagerly. Besides Bay and her companions there were only a few other people at the table. A young gentleman wearing a suit sat across from Bay, there was also an older woman, and a middle aged woman who looked as if she might start crying at any moment.

Mallory suddenly appeared and sat at the table beside Brien. "What are you all staring at the food for? Dig in! Oh wait where is my mind today?" Mallory laughed, and shook her head as if she had just heard a very funny joke, "let us bow our heads and thank the Lord," she said. When they said grace Mallory picked up the plate of chicken, put a slice on her plate and past it on. She did this with all the dishes until everyone's plate was full.

There was silence at the table as everyone started eating. Brien had been right, the food was delicious! Bay ate quickly at first, but then slowed down to saver the flavor. The gentleman in the suit finished first.

"Lovely meal, madam," he said in a perfect English accent, "but I mush be off, I
have an engagement I'm running late for."

"Well you have fun dearie," Mallory said. The gentleman nodded to everyone at the table then left.

"So, what have you been up to lately Brien?" Mallory asked, as she cleaned off her plate and helped herself to seconds.

"Not much," Brien lied, "I have finished my book, I have been trying to get it published, so I've been traveling around, looking for different companies. And I was in the neighborhood so I decided to spend the night here."

"You left quite suddenly last time," Mallory said.

"Yes something important came up, I had to leave right away. I'm sorry I couldn't say good-bye."

"No harm done dear," Mallory said waving her hand in the air. The older woman suddenly stood up.

"That was very good Mallory," the woman said, her face was strict, and she spoke as if she were a teacher complementing a student. "I'm going to bed now."

"Sleep well!" Mallory called. The woman nodded and disappeared up the stairs. Lex had finished his supper and was

120

helping himself to a slice of cake, Bay followed suit.

"Is the cake any good sweetie?" Mallory asked Bay.

"It's great!" Bay said truthfully licking the icing from the corner of her mouth. Mallory beamed with pride and cut a piece herself.

"Would you like a piece dear?" Mallory asked kindly to the other woman. She looked up with surprise and stared at the chocolate cake, as if wondering what it was. "Here, you look like you need something sweet in your mouth." Mallory put a slightly larger slice on the woman's plate. She picked up her fork and took a small bite, as if she were afraid the cake might be poison.

Everyone finished at the same time, including the frightened looking girl. Mallory let out a small burp and chuckled to herself.

"Well I can get the dishes later," Mallory said, "Let's go into the living room for some tea and wine." Everyone stood up and followed Mallory to the living room. Bay sat down next to her father on the couch. The woman sat in a rocking chair by the fire, and Brien and Mallory sat on a love seat on the other side of the coffee table.

Mallory poured out some tea. Bay took hers gratefully and sipped the warm liquid. Lex also took some. Brien excepted a glass of brandy, when Mallory offered some to the woman she quickly shook her head no, and touched her stomach. Bay noticed that it was slightly bloated and realized that she was with child. The woman took tea instead and stared at the fire thoughtfully.

"Have you had any luck Brien?" Mallory asked.

"Not yet, but I'm still hopeful."

"That's good, don't give up, that's what my mother always said, and that's what I said when the Inn was having trouble, and look how well that worked out!"

"So business is good?" Brien asked.

"Oh yes! Shireville has become a bit of a historical landmark, a lot of people come in to see our old town, tourism you know. And I have been making some extra money selling my paintings."

"Are you an artist?" Bay asked. Mallory chuckled a little.

"Well, I do some painting and sketching, I guess you could call me that."

"Did you paint these?" Bay asked pointing to the pictures on the wall.

"Yes I'm very fond of water color."

"They are beautiful paintings," Bay said. Mallory blushed and sipped her tea. Everyone was silent for a moment, as if waiting for someone else to start the conversation. Mallory of course, obliged.

"What about you dear?" the pregnant woman looked up startled. "You haven't said a word all evening," Mallory said, "At least oblige us with your name."

"Constance," the girl whispered.

"Such a pretty name!" Mallory said, "what brings you to Shireville? Not that it's any of my business, I'm just trying to break the ice." The woman finally gave Mallory a small smile.

"That's all right." Constance said, "I'm going to have a baby, and the father has been away for awhile, so I'm going to meet him and give the news."

"Congratulations!" Mallory said, "you will love being a mother, it's the most wonderful feeling in the world. At least I think so."

"Do you have children?" Constance asked.

"Oh yes, a son. He was in the great war, now he trains young solders. He is actually retiring next year, says he is going to open a shop here and start a family, that will be wonderful. I miss little ones, and I'm afraid I have been nagging Nathan to give me some grandchildren lately," Mallory laughed. Constance smiled again, she had a very pretty smile, Bay hoped she would do it more often.

"You will like having children," Lex said, "I thought my life began when I was born, but it didn't really begin until I had Bay." Bay smiled and Lex put his arm around her.

"That shows you are a good father," Mallory said.

"I hope so," Lex said. Bay yawned and laid her head on his shoulder.

"My it is late," Mallory said, as if Bay's yawn was the cue to check her watch. "Everyone get a good nights sleep," Mallory said. Everyone stood up and went to the stairs. Mallory went to the dinning room to collect the dishes.

"How about I give you a hand?" Brien said.

"No, no dear, you go sleep," Mallory said shooing him. Brien laughed and dodged her hand.

"You know I don't like sleeping, I insist," Brien entered the dinning room and began picking up the dishes. Lex and Bay made their way upstairs, with Constance behind them. Her room was next to theirs.

"If you need any help, just ask," Lex said, "I know the discomforts of pregnancy."

"Oh, have you been pregnant before?" Constance asked. They both laughed cheerfully. Bay found it hard to believe that the quiet woman downstairs had a since of humor.

"I guess your right," Lex said, "but I'm still here if you need assistance." Constance giggled.

"Thank you. I'm sorry about the remark, but I couldn't resist."

"Don't worry, I needed a good laugh." They both stared into each others eyes, it just takes a small moment like this for a persons heart to connect, and Lex found that Constance was a very beautiful woman. She had long blond hair, and lovely green eyes. They stood there for a moment just watching each other. Lex blinked and came back to Earth.

"Good night," Lex said.

"You too," Constance closed her door, Lex hesitated then went into his own room.

Bay had dressed in her pajamas and had crawled into bed. Lex realized that he too was very tired. He removed his shirt and laid down beside Bay. Bay huddled close to him, Lex stroked her hair lovingly.

"Good night angel, I love you."

"I love you too dad." Then they were both asleep.

123

Chapter Twelve

Darc sat in his living room still as a cat. The only light on in the house was the one in the bedroom upstairs. All though there was no one up there.

A shot gun lay across Darc's lap, his finger was resting on the trigger. His wife and three kids had gone to his mother's house. A few hours after Ink had left a strange car had pulled into town, Darc had been watching the road and he immediately recognized Rivan, who had three men with him.

Rivan had gone into an Inn first, the keeper told him that he had seen a buggy come into town, but they had eaten at a restaurant across the street. When Rivan asked if they were still in town the man said he didn't know.

Rivan had gone to the restaurant and asked one of the waiters if he had seen two men and a girl come in. Darc spied on them from the kitchen, he owned the restaurant, and had already told his employs what to say if Rivan came.

"Yes sir, I remember them," the waiter, his name was Cody, told Rivan.

"Did you see if they left town or not?" Rivan asked, he

held up some money for Cody to see. Darc had always figured Rivan to be a briber.

"They stayed, they had asked me if Stanley Darc still lived here, I told him he did. They said that they were old friends, so I gave them the address. I think they are still there." Rivan gave Cody the money and left the restaurant.

When he was gone Darc had called his wife and told her to go to his mother's house. He closed the shop early and went home, he knew Rivan would be watching the house, and would probably wait until dark to attack.

When eight o'clock came and Rivan had not shown up, Darc had decided to call the police just in case. The minutes past by slowly, there was a sheriff in town, but the police force were a few miles away in the big cities, if the sheriff wanted back up it could be awhile.

Darc felt tense, he turned at every sound, and jumped when he saw a shadow move. But Rivan was obviously taking his time, he might not even come until midnight.

But Darc did not have to wait that long. He heard a loud snap, as someone managed to break open the lock on his door. Darc stood up and held his gun at the ready. He was hidden inside his bedroom, anything that came through the door would be shot.

For a moment there was silence, then Darc heard voices, he came closer to the door to hear what they said.

"Ink is probably still here," this was Rivan's voice, "Fargo, search the rooms down here, Jacob, search the rooms upstairs, I'll come with you. Remember to take them alive, we end this here and now."

"We'll end something," Jacob said, "I want revenge off that brat who set my back on fire and cut me." Darc couldn't hear Rivan's reply, there were heavy footsteps as they made their way upstairs.

Darc opened his door so slowly and carefully that someone would simply think it was a draft. The one called Fargo was looking at any hiding places in the living room.

Darc took his shoes off, Fargo turned his back and

opened the door that led to the basement.

Quick as a fox, yet quiet as a mouse, Darc raced swiftly across the room and hit Fargo in the back of the head with the butt of his gun. Fargo let out a mere grunt and fell forward, unconscious. Darc grabbed his shirt before he hit the ground. Darc laid him on the stairs and shut the door. That would hold him for a while.

Darc turned and walked quietly up the stairs to take care of Rivan and Jacob. Jacob was in the first room. Darc couldn't help but smile as the man sneaked up to the bed and threw back the covers revealing some pillows. Darc had laid them out earlier to fool anyone into thinking someone was sleeping in the beds.

Darc rushed forward and hit Jacob over the head. The man groaned and turned, Darc slammed the gun across his face and Jacob fell back on the bed with a soft thump. Two down, one to go, Darc thought pleasingly. He left the room, Rivan had gone down the hall to the room that had a light on. Darc dropped the stealth mood and threw open the door. Rivan stood there, his hand reached out as if to grab the door knob. Darc pointed the gun at his head. Rivan only stared as if he had expected this.

"Back up," Darc demanded. Rivan took a few steps back. "You have better remember who I am," Darc said threateningly.

"One-ear," Rivan said, "I don't know your real name, I'm afraid a nickname was necessary." Darc felt his face turn red, he gripped the gun tightly, he was a proud man and he was not willing to let Rivan get away with that.

"I'm sending you to jail where you belong," Darc said.

"No you won't, One-ear," Rivan sneered. Darc cocked his gun and glared at him.

"And how are you going to stop me?" Darc demanded.

"Oh, I won't stop you at all," Rivan said innocently, "but he might." Before Darc could turn to face his attacker he was struck over the head. Darc fell forward and hit the ground, everything in the room seemed to spin as Darc struggled to remain conscious.

The gun was taken from his hands, and all he could think was: the third man, I'm a bloody idiot, I forgot the third man! Someone grabbed Darc and binded his hands tightly.

Things came into focus slowly. Darc sat on the ground with his back against the wall. Rivan now stood in front of him pointing the gun at his head. The third man that Darc had forgotten stood beside Rivan with his arms crossed, like a loyal bodyguard.

"Now, you are going to do what I ask," Rivan said, "I'm sure your family is not far, perhaps your sons will like to join us, or your lovely wife." Darc tried to lunge at Rivan, but remembered that his hands were tied.

"There is no need to strain yourself," Rivan said teasingly, "We will not have to disturb your family tonight, if you do as I say."

"Fine," Darc spat, "I have no love for Ink, but I'm not a friend for you either, I shall only do it for my family. But I swear on God's name that if you harm them I will hunt you down and murder you, every last one of you." Rivan smiled cruelly.

"There will be no need for that, but I fear we digress. Where is Ink?"

"He left here yesterday, he mentioned Shireville. It's a few miles up the road."

"I know where it is," Rivan said frowning, "what would Ink want there?" he mumbled to himself.

"I don't know, probably that book of his," Darc said, even though Rivan had not asked him.

"Yes," Rivan whispered to himself, "that dreadful book." Rivan straightened up and looked at Darc. "Very well One-ear, I am a man of my word." Rivan turned and left the room. The third man stepped forward and struck Darc across the head. Darc groaned and fell to the floor. He was struck again and he knew only darkness.

Rivan threw water over Jacob and Fargo, waking them. "One-ear is unconscious," Rivan told them, "It should keep him out of our way for a few days. Ink is in Shireville."

"How do we know the one eared freak wasn't lying, eh?" Fargo asked. He reached up and scratched his bald head nervously.

"Don't worry, I can since a lie on a man, One-ear was telling the truth. He wouldn't take a chance on his family anyway." Rivan let out an evil laugh, "that's what I love about humans, doesn't matter who they are they all have a weakness. Come, I am curious as to what Ink will be wanting in Shireville. Of all places!"

Chapter Thirteen

Lex found that he was sleeping lightly, his mind was too restless to sleep deeply. When Brien entered the room Lex opened his eyes a little but did not stir, there was no need to start a conversation in the middle of the night, they might wake Bay.

Brien pulled off his shirt, but did not get into the second bed. Instead Brien studied Lex for a moment, then walked to the other side of the room. Lex sat up in bed peering through the darkness to see what he was up to. Brien went to a corner of the room and bent down on his knees. Some moonlight fell through the window so Lex could make out what his friend was doing.

Brien pulled a knife from his pocket and began cutting away at the carpet edge, where the carpet met the wall. Lex frowned and leaned closer. Brien cut the carpet away and pulled it off revealing the wooden floor underneath. Using the knife Brien pried the nails off the wood and set the pieces aside. When it was done Brien removed something small and flat from the hollow under the boards.

Lex couldn't help but smile when he saw the leather bound manuscript. Lex gave himself a good, mental kick, he should have known! Brien Ink did not travel two countries for nothing. Brien replaced the boards, and the carpet. He put the manuscript in a secret compartment in his bag and got into bed.

"Nice hiding place," Lex whispered when Brien had pulled the covers over himself.

"Go to sleep you spying cad." Both men chuckled and closed their eyes.

***

Bay was the first to wake the next morning. She felt wonderfully refreshed, and well rested. Bay quickly dressed and went downstairs. Mallory was also an early bird. Bacon, eggs, toast, pancakes, porridge, and coffee were all laid out on the table nice and hot.

"This looks great Mallory!" Bay said taking a seat.

"Thank you dear. Please eat, Madam Geoffrey has her breakfast in bed, and the gentleman Richard you met last night was out a little late, so we can't wait for breakfast can we?"

Bay sat at the table and helped herself to breakfast. One pancake drowned in syrup, and covered in butter, two slices of bacon, and a piece of jellied toast. But when she tried to pour herself a cup of coffee Mallory caught her and took it away.

"Please, I'm old enough!" Bay said disappointed. Mallory giggled.

"To much caffeine for a small system, you have enough energy to get you through the day." Bay got a glass of orange juice instead. Bay ate by herself, at first. Constance appeared next though.

"Hello dear, do you need something to settle your stomach? I know all about morning sickness," Mallory said, she always seemed to appear from the kitchen just as someone came downstairs.

"No I'm fine," Constance said smiling, "I have a strong stomach." Bay watched with interest as Constance helped herself to everything on the table, except eggs, Bay couldn't blame her, she had never cared much for eggs either.

"Did you sleep well Bay?" Constance asked as she put another bite of pancake in her mouth.

"Great," Bay said, she was almost surprised Constance remembered her name, what had happened to the shy weak woman last night? Maybe she just needed a long rest, it really was amazing what a good nights sleep could do for someone.

"Where are you traveling to?" Constance asked, "I noticed your mother isn't traveling with you."

"No," Bay said shaking her head, "my mom past away almost thirteen years ago, when I was two." Constance gasped.

"Oh, I'm so sorry Bay, I didn't know."

"It's all right, I don't remember her a lot. I don't know if it would be better to know her, or not, but this is how it is." Bay shrugged her shoulders and drank her juice.

"Well, I'm glad I didn't hurt your feelings. Where are you going?"

"I'm not to sure," Bay said, "Brien does most of the travel plans."

"What about your father?" Constance asked. Bay caught a certain tone in her voice, but she couldn't tell what it meant.

"My dad is called Alexander, but everyone calls him Lex. He is a friend of Brien, we are just accompanying him."

"Do you like it?" Constance asked. Bay couldn't help but laugh out loud.

"It has it's highs and lows, but it's been very, very interesting."

"You will have to tell me about it sometime," Constance said smiling. Bay nodded.

"I will," her tone said that it was a promise. Brien came down next, followed by Lex. Lex sat down beside Constance, Brien beside Bay. They finished breakfast, but didn't leave the table, everyone was deep in conversation, Mallory had joined them as well.

Richard suddenly stumbled into the room, his eyes were bloodshot, and his clothes were baggy. His hair was messy and

131

uncombed. Mallory stared at him and shook her head as if ashamed.

"Richard, there is a child here!" Mallory stood up and poured a cup of coffee. Richard fell into one of the chairs with a groan.

"If you feel so bad why didn't you stay in bed?" Mallory demanded, she now sounded angry.

"God, what a night..." Richard mumbled.

"If you thought that was bad wait until I'm done with you," Mallory said. She held up the cup and helped Richard get it down his throat. "I said, 'have fun,' not get drunk and come in here like an idiot, embarrassing me in front of the guests!"

Richard could only grumble in response. When he had drained the coffee, Mallory took his arm and they disappeared into the kitchen. A moment later there was a loud splash, and loud voices arguing. Mallory appeared once again dragging Richard, who was soaked in cold water. Bay couldn't help but giggle. Lex just shook his head.

Mallory took Richard upstairs scolding him, like a mother scolding her child.

Everyone at the table laughed despite themselves. Bay settled back in her chair and smiled, finally peace, Rivan was not there, and the only thing to worry about was James. Bay wondered where he could be.

"Well we need to get back to our room," Brien said, "We shall see you later Miss Constance." Constance smiled and nodded to them. Bay and Lex followed him back to the room. When they entered Brien locked the door, and closed the curtains.

"What's going on?" Bay asked.

Brien went to his bag and pulled out the manuscript with a pleased smile on his face.

"You sneak!" Bay cried, "It was here all along, you didn't tell us."

"I said it was a secret," Brien said, "Anyway, this is the last one, the first thing we need to do is make more copies, then send it to a publishing company."

"Is there a printing press in Shireville?" Lex asked.

"I think so, but I will ask Mallory to make sure," Brien said. They stood up, Brien put the manuscript in a small bag that he could carry over his shoulder. They left the room and went downstairs, once there they bumped into Constance.

"Off for some sight seeing?" Constance asked.

"Something like that," Lex said.

"Mind if I join you?"

"Sure, I mean if Brien doesn't mind," Lex said. Brien studied lex then smiled knowingly.

"Not at all." The four of them left the Inn and walked out onto the street. It was busy with people going to work, and doing their shopping. Linking arms they walked down the street together staring at the shops and admiring the old fashioned style of the village.

Brien stopped a man selling flowers loaded on his cart. They said something in German, the man with the cart nodded his head and pointed down the road. Brien thanked him and went on.

"What did you say?" Bay asked.

"I asked him where the printing press was, there is one at the newspaper."

"What do you need a printing press for?" Constance asked.

"I just need to have something copied," Brien said casually. The crowd seemed to thicken. Bay was almost ran over by a tall man walking past them.

"Ouch!" Bay cried out. The man glanced down, their eyes locked together, and Bay thought she might faint in shock and fear. Rivan cold eyes looked into hers. Bay gasped, without a word she turned and ran back to her companions who had gotten a few feet away.

"Brien!" Bay clutched his jacket tightly, "It's him Brien, they found us!" With a sharp turn Brien saw Rivan pushing through the crowd towards them. They had arrived sometime in the night. Since early morning Rivan and his henchmen had been searching different hotels, asking around.

Brien grabbed Bay's hand and Lex's arm. Lex grabbed

Constance and with a great tug, Brien pulled them forward through the crowd. The bag slipped off Brien's shoulder onto Bay's arm.

"I've got it," She whispered. Bay pulled the bag on her shoulder and they all jogged down the street, with Rivan close behind. A man pushing a cart came towards them, Bay went one way, Brien went the other. They were suddenly separated.

Bay stared in horror at her empty hand. She searched the crowd desperately trying to find Brien. "Dad! Brien! Where are you?" Bay yelled. She turned suddenly and saw Rivan lunge at her. Bay screamed and ran. Rivan came after her.

Bay pushed through the crowd off the sidewalk. She entered a small yard, up ahead was a large catholic church built in a castle form, with a bell tower and everything. Rivan came after her once again, his fingers brushed the bag. Bay pulled away and ran inside the stone chapel.

The large building was quiet, muffled voices of the priest were the only sounds. Bay ran down the isle between the pews to the alter where the sermon was held. One of the priest spotted her and grabbed her arm gently.

"Young lady, this is a house of God, please do not..."

"You have to help!" Bay said panting, "there is a man after me..." The doors suddenly opened and Rivan stepped in, he immediately saw Bay and ran towards her.

"Please call help!" Bay screamed, she turned and ran through a door behind the alter.

"See here!" the priest tried to stop Rivan but Rivan merely pushed him out of the way and followed Bay through the door.

Bay entered a long hallway, the walls were lined with stain glass windows, and doors. Bay ran down the hall, her footsteps echoing off the walls, a second pair of footsteps echoed after hers. Bay threw open the door at the end of the passage. This was the entrance to a tall flight of stairs. Not caring where they lead, Bay closed the door and ran upward.

Rivan opened the door and climbed after her. Bay's legs began to throb from the strain of running uphill. Her ribcage screamed in pain, and Bay was gasping for breath, Rivan was getting closer.

Bay screamed in horror when he tried to grab her leg. With

a burst of precious energy Bay pulled forward and continued up the never ending stairs, the backpack that held the manuscript bumped against her side.

Bay saw a door up ahead, she had reached the top. Bay grabbed the handle and threw it open. She slammed it shut behind her, there was a latch to lock it. Bay pulled it forward. Rivan pushed against the door, but Bay locked it before he could enter.

Bay fell onto her back gasping for sweet air, her lungs moved rapidly, and her heart beat as though it were still running, Bay could hear it pounding, though she didn't know if it was her heart, or Rivan fighting the door.

Very slowly her heart slowed, the pain subsided, and she breathed freely again. Bay felt a cool wind on her face. She opened her eyes and gasped in horror.

She was in the bell tower. The large metal bell hung above her, still and silent. The tower was square shaped, and small. Bay crawled to the edge and saw there were no railings just a sloping roof leading downward to the ground, over a hundred feet below. Bay felt dizzy, she backed away from the edge and curled up under the bell. Rivan was still on the other side of the door trying to break through. Bay saw that the latch was starting to give, it was old, well built, but still old.

But what did it matter? Bay was trapped, there was no where to go, Rivan would break through the door, steal the manuscript, and probably throw her out of the tower. Bay laid her head on her knees and began to weep softly, she didn't want to cry, she didn't want Rivan to have the satisfaction of seeing tears on her face before she died.

But they came never the less, and Bay let them fall. She looked up at the sky. It was a glorious blue, only a few fluffy clouds floated across it, like soft pillows floating in the ocean. Bay wanted to curl up on a cloud and float away from the tower, she wanted to fly across the never ending sky, and land safely in her father's arms.

Bay looked back at the door. Rivan had managed to bend the latch and open the door a few inches. Bay suddenly remembered something. Reaching into her pocket she pulled out the chocolate bar that the man on the train had given her. She wiped away her tears and opened the wrapper, the slightly melted chocolate tasted wonderful, and relaxed her tired body, a little anyway. It calmed her enough to think straight. She finished the chocolate and put the wrapper in her pocket. She looked at the now shattering door, then at the towers edge.

Then a familiar line entered her memory, 'continue to give hope.' It was from Brien's letter, the one that had brought her into this adventure, continue to give hope. Bay looked up at the bell, then she glanced down at the crowd of people below. Brien and Lex must be there, looking for her. Bay wiped the tears from her cheeks and stood up. It wasn't over yet, there was still a chance, just a glimmer of hope.

The cord that rang the bell hung loosely in the corner. Bay picked it up in her hands. The rope was very thick and heavy, it would take a lot of strength, but in her heart, Bay knew she could do it.

Bay gripped the rope tightly, one arm over the other, with a deep breath, Bay gave a a large pull. The bell shuddered and waved a little, it was just a shiver, but it had moved.

"Come on," Bay whispered. Rivan had gotten the door open a few more inches, there wasn't much time. Bay lifted herself off the floor clutching the rope, while still pulling on it. The bell move and knocked the gong in the middle. It wasn't very loud, or hard, but down below people glanced up to see why the bell had moved.

"Third times the charm," Bay said. With that she put all her energy, body weight, and will power into pulling the cord. This time the rope came downward, the bell rocked and struck the gong. A loud clear sound echoed through the town.

Bay laughed with pleasure as she flew upward and downward with the cord, her feet actually leaving the ground. The bell rang out again, then again. Bay let go and fell to the ground. She smiled and went to the edge of the tower. A crowd of people were forming at the church staring up at the tower, wondering who had rang the bell, and for what purpose. Bay leaned out as far as she dared and waved her arms.

"BRIEN! LEX!" She screamed out with all her might. She was too far up to see if they had seen her, but it was too late now. With a crash, Rivan broke the door down and came out into the tower. Bay gasped and stood up, clutching the bag in her hands.

"Well done, you rang the bell. Who do you think will come to your rescue?" Rivan asked walking towards her.

"Who do you think?" Bay said forcefully, feeling mad, and sarcastic. Rivan laughed and shook his head.

"You can't count on other people kid, in the end you are alone, no matter what." Bay shook her head. Bay glanced at the sky, and thought about her mother, in her heart Bay knew she would be proud of her. Rivan only chuckled.

"You have a lot of spirit Bay Paxon, I must admit that I admired that about you. It's a shame really." Rivan now stood in front of her, but Bay was no longer afraid of his cold eyes, there was no fear in her heart.

"Give me the manuscript and I might let you live." Bay let a small smile form on her lips.

"You want it? Go and get it," With that Bay threw the bag over the edge of the tower. Rivan reached forward to grab it but the bag fell through the air into the crowd below.

Rivan turned and glared at her, but Bay only glared back, feeling a since of pride. Rivan advanced on her. He grabbed her shoulders and pulled her towards the edge of the tower, Bay struggled, but Rivan was now the only thing keeping Bay from falling to her death.

"Let's see if you can fly," Rivan said. Bay felt his hands release her shoulders. She felt nothing but air as she began to fall. She fell backwards towards the ground, through the cool May air. It happened in slow motion, it was almost peaceful. Then suddenly her back struck the wall, and Bay hung upside down from the tower. Looking up Bay saw Lex clutching her leg with both hands, his face was red, and his muscles pulsed, but he had her. His little girl in his hands.

Lex winced and pulled, Bay felt herself traveling upward. She reached upward, Lex yanked and Bay was lying safely on the floor. Lex stared at her with wide eyes, his hands

137

trembling. Bay had never seen her father cry, and when that tear fell down his cheek she burst into tears and they embraced each other, never letting go.

Brien was behind them. He and Rivan stood facing each other. Fist flew through the air, they struck each other and fought fiercely. Brien reached forward and grabbed Rivan's shirt, Brien spun in a circle like an ice skater and let go.

Rivan hit the floor, but he skidded and began falling. He fell through the air, but no one grabbed him to stop the terrible fall. Rivan flew through the air, down below people screamed in horror. He struck the ground at full force, and was dead.

Brien stared at his hands and backed away from the tower's edge, his body trembling. It was never easy to kill a man, even if it was your purpose.

Brien sat on the ground, he felt like laughing and crying all at the same time, but his face remained blank. Lex approached him, and Bay wrapped her arms around him, and kissed his cheek.

Brien blinked and gently hugged her back. "Maybe it's better this way," he whispered. Lex nodded, then Bay nodded.

"What are we going to do?" Brien said, "I'll be arrested."

"For what?" Lex asked. Brien stared at him.

"Murder."

"Murder? I didn't see a murder, did you Bay?" the girl shook her blond head. "I saw Rivan stumble and fall off the edge, it was an accident, am I right?"

"That's what I saw," Bay said putting on her most innocent face. Brien stared at them for a moment then smiled and bowed his head.

"Come on Ink," Lex said. He grabbed Brien's arm and pulled him to his feet, though none of them felt like walking, their legs trembled too much. They made their way back down the stairs to the church once again. Bay quickly explained that she had thrown the manuscript off the tower. They jogged back outside to find the bag before someone else did, but someone all ready had.

James stood at the entrance holding up the bag, and smiling

at them, "did you drop something?" he asked. Bay laughed and grabbed him in a tight hug.

"I was so worried, what happened?" Bay asked. James had jumped off the ferry in order to get help. But when he had gotten the police, Rivan and his men had already tracked down the train they had taken. James couldn't leave for Germany until that night, so he stole a car, and drove all night, and morning to reach Shireville.

"I'm sorry I had to leave you," James said, "Is everyone all right?"

"Just a little shaken," Lex said. Police suddenly appeared. Rivan's body was taken away, and everyone was held back for questioning. The entire story came out in Brien's words that midmorning at the church. In the end they gave the story in the tower. Since Rivan was dead, and Bay and Lex were the only witnesses they were released without charges.

Constance found them in the crowd as they went back to the Shireville Inn. Once everyone was sitting in Mallory's living room with hot cups of tea, and brandy, the story was told again. Bay and Lex sat beside each other wrapped in a quilt, with Constance sitting beside Lex. Brien sat before everyone, with James and Mallory beside him, even Madam Geoffrey came down to listen to their amazing story.

In the end Constance's eyes were wide, and everyone was silent. Constance broke the silence by saying, "may I read your story Brien?"

"Why?" Brien asked. He had the manuscript on his lap, like a well loved cat.

"Because," Constance suddenly smiled mysteriously, "I work for a publishing house in London, I am one of the chief editors."

Bay smiled and hugged Lex closer. You couldn't guarantee happy endings, but sometimes they are inevitable.

EPILOGUE

Bay sat in a rocking chair on the porch of their new house, with Brien beside her. Both were silent and staring at the road, as if it were the only thing in the world.

Cold September wind blew across the yard scattering the newly fallen leaves. Bay shivered and buttoned her jacket. It was early morning, the sun had just crawled out from behind the horizon, making the Autumn air even colder, but nether of them made a move to go back inside. The sound of a motor suddenly reached their ears. They both looked eagerly, but it was simply a man going out for a ride to town. They both sighed with impatience and leaned back into the chair.

Lex had bought the new house with some money he had been saving for such an emergency. Bay loved the house, it had plenty of rooms, and even a large attic used for storing books. You would often hear the clicking of Brien's typewriter from underneath the floor, as he busily wrote down new stories on the small desk that he had moved up there. It was no longer an attic, but a library, and study.

Brien had decided to take a year or two off traveling. Though he would be leaving next June to go to America. After all, a newly formed country should have plenty of new stories

141

waiting to be written. In the mean time Lex had gladly offered Brien a room in the new house, an Brien excepted, he proved to be very useful around the house, especially when a baby was expected.

Constance had lied to them about the baby's father, he had died, but they were not married, so he left her nothing in the will. In desperation Constance had gone to Germany to find some long lost relatives to help her. Instead she came back to Whipshire with Lex, they planned to be married in October after the baby was born, which would be any day now. Bay knew she would love having a sibling, and a mother. Constance had told her that she would not replace her real mother, but she hoped they could be good friends. Bay loved her all the more for that.

It was now almost four months after the Church Tower Incident, as Brien put it. Bay had put the past behind her, she had never felt so happy in all her life. It all led to that moment in time where Brien and Bay sat on the porch staring at the road. Their patience was finally rewarded.

The sound of a motor reached their ears once again, they looked up eagerly and saw a large white delivery van appear from around the corner. They both jumped up and raced each other to the drive. The driver stepped out of the car holding a very large, and very heavy package.

Brien let Bay beat him to the package. She signed the paper, and together they carried it back into the house. Brien set it down on the kitchen table. Bay shouted out, "Wake up! It's here everybody!" Footsteps echoed through the house. Lex appeared holding Constance's arm. Her belly was swollen to the point where she waddled, and had trouble moving around. Bay placed her ear to the stomach to hear the infant squirm inside. She kissed the belly then kissed her father. Everyone had decided that if it was to be a boy they would name it Brien. But if it was a girl they would call it Kira, after Bay's mother. Deep in her heart, Bay knew it was a girl, Constance did too.

The door suddenly opened and James appeared, "is it here?" he asked. Everyone nodded. James had continued to work with Delon and Cornelia. He had rebuilt the stables, and took care of the horses. But he would be moving on soon, he had gotten a contract with a construction company, he was going to be a carpenter.

Brien stared at the box, like a child on Christmas morning. Everyone sat at the table eagerly.

"Open it!" Bay said, her heart was filled with excitement. Brien pulled out a pocket knife and cut away the tape and twine. He threw open the lid and stared at the contents within. With trembling hands, Brien reached into the box and pulled out his book. The thick pages were covered with hardback, stamped across the front in lovely letters were the words:

The Lost Manuscript

By Brien Ink

A tear slid down Brien's cheek as he stared at his finally published work, the greatest feeling for a writer to finally see their book in print, so that the world could read their stories. Everyone reached into the box and pulled out their own copy, complements of the company. Constance had loved the book, she had to pull a few strings but she had it published.

Brien ran his fingers over the cover lovingly. Constance smiled, "we will be expected you to get to work," she said teasingly, "the sales have gone great, and the company is willing to publish you again. So don't think you can just run off to America and leave us dangling." Brien chuckled.

"I wouldn't dream of it," He said. While everyone pitched in to make a celebration breakfast, Bay sneaked outside back to the porch. Under her arm she held her copy of the manuscript, and a blank notebook.

Sitting down on the rocking chair, Bay studied the two booklets in front of her. She gently set down Brien's book on a side table, there would be plenty of time for reading.

143

Bay opened up her notebook. The thick, white pages stared at her waiting to be filled. Bay pulled out her ink pen and opened the cap. The tip hovered over the paper for a moment, as if scared to touch the lovely clean paper.

But Bay only smiled. Her heart was swelled with happiness, the sun shined in the clear blue sky, beginning a new day. Bay took a deep breath, she placed her pen on the paper and began to write.

CPSIA information can be obtained
at www.ICGtesting.com
Printed in the USA
LVOW07s1511050217
523247LV00002B/182/P